THE NAVAJO
BROTHERS
▲ AND ▼
THE STOLEN HERD

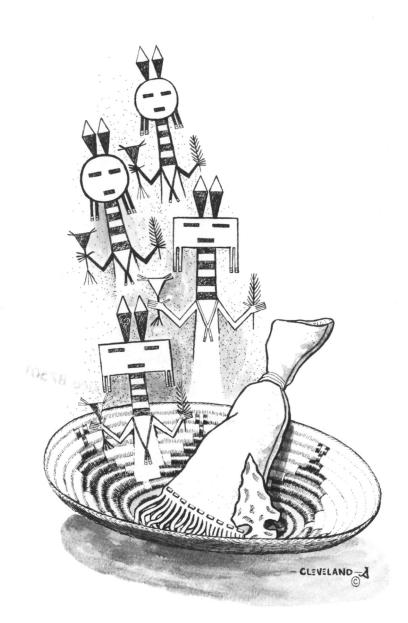

THE NAVAJO BROTHERS ▲ AND ▼ THE STOLEN HERD

Maurine Grammer

Illustrations by Fred Cleveland

Foreword by Jack Rushing

R·E·D
CRANE
BOOKS

Santa Fe

Foreword copyright © 1992 by Jack Rushing
Cover and text drawings copyright © 1992 by Fred Cleveland
First Edition
Manufactured in the United States of America
Cover and text design by Joanna Hill

Library of Congress Cataloging-in-Publication Data
Grammer, Maurine.
    The Navajo brothers and the stolen herd / Maurine Grammer;
foreword by Jack Rushing; illustrated by Fred Cleveland.—1st ed.
        p.   cm.
    Summary: Chee and Pahee, teenage Navajo brothers in New
Mexico, lose their family's herd of sheep to thieves and attempt to
get it back.
    ISBN 1-878610-23-6
    1. Navajo Indians—Juvenile fiction. [1. Navjo Indians—Fiction.
2. Indians of North America—Fiction. 3. New Mexico—Fiction.]
I. Cleveland, Fred, ill. II. Title.
PZ7.G7656Nav 1992
[Fic]—dc20   92-15018
                                                          CIP
                                                          AC

Red Crane Books
826 Camino de Monte Rey
Santa Fe, New Mexico 87501

CONTENTS

FOREWORD

*The chief glory of every people arises from
its authors.*

Samuel Johnson, 1755

Each of us knows special books that, when
finished, leave one wanting more and sad that the story's
spell has ended. You know your special books, for you have
given or shared them with family and friends. These books,
with their attendant glories, are passed to new readers
with heartfelt words of praise and the rich memory of your
own first reading of these special stories.

When you put down *The Navajo Brothers and the Stolen Herd*, you will appreciate an ancient culture, understand
many of its beliefs, and experience the powerful pull of an
indomitable land few know and visit.

Maurine Grammer has been gathering the background
information for this special book almost from the first day
she came to New Mexico, as a young bride, sixty years ago.
From her early childhood in Missouri, through her college
days in Missouri and Wyoming, then as a gifted teacher,
and a generous friend to many, many Native Americans,
Hispanics, and Anglos, she has always been a keen listener, an intelligent, truthful observer, respectful of
tradition and values, and a master storyteller.

Soon after arriving in Albuquerque, Maurine and her husband David visited new Navajo friends living on the Puertecito Reservation (now called the Alamo Band Indian Reservation) in west central New Mexico. Puertecito is rugged, mountainous country with wide canyons and few people. These "lands of evening" captivated the Grammers; they returned often; the land and its people captivate Maurine Grammer to this day.

Erna Fergusson was an internationally famous author who wrote about the Southwest and Latin America in more than a dozen books. Writing of New Mexico, she might have had in mind Puertecito's powerful hold on the few who know, or have experienced it, when she wrote that the land "is too strong, too indomitable for most people. Those who can stand it had to learn that man does not modify this country, it transforms him, deeply."

Few live on or near Puertecito. Few visit or know of it. Little has been written about this vast country; perhaps the best known writer was Agnes Morley Cleveland, who, in her 1941 memoir, *No Life for a Lady*, describes ranch life before statehood.

The Alamo Reservation is rugged mountains, windswept mesas, and the canyon "lands of the evening." On a map, Alamo is readily identifiable, like a desert oasis, on the large, virtually barren space that is west central New Mexico. Yet this country is anything but barren. In this country, the past is ever present. The immense landscape is harsh; and the passersby such as the Anasazi, the Mimbreño, the Spanish, Confederates and Yankees, lawmen such as Elfego Baca, vaqueros, cowboys, miners, lumberjacks, astronauts, railroads, progress, and the Dinè—all have been "transformed" by this country. To my knowledge, only one other area of New Mexico, the Bootheel, is so prominent (and appears as vacant) on maps, is equally remote, has had so little written about it, and remains "too strong, too indomitable for most people," to quote Erna Fergusson.

Maurine Grammer knew this Alamo Dinotah (home land) from the time she and her husband first came to New Mexico. She has a special love for its people, their culture, and the land. For sixty years, she has been teacher, friend, foster parent, trader, banker, supplier, artistic encourager, collector of tales, and trusted adviser to the Navajo.

Maurine Grammer draws on years of experience, patient listening, study, friendships, and direct knowledge in writing *The Navajo Brothers and the Stolen Herd*. To the generations of her students who were fortunate to hear her marvelous stories, as I was, *The Navajo Brothers and the Stolen Herd* is her crowning achievement and a lasting tribute to this remarkable woman.

The Navajo Brothers and the Stolen Herd presents Navajo beliefs, customs, values, and knowledge that all readers will understand. The Navajo search for harmony immerses the reader in a time-honored contest of good versus evil set in the rugged Alamo country. When you finish reading this classic, you will understand why Maurine Grammer is a keen listener, an inspiring teacher, and a gifted storyteller.

I gave *The Navajo Brothers and the Stolen Herd* to a good friend. This friend sent me the following translated portion of the Navajo Night Chant, as an appropriate thank you, for sharing this classic story:

> *May it be beautiful before me.*
> *May it be beautiful behind me.*
> *May it be beautiful below me.*
> *May it be beautiful above me.*
> *May it be beautiful all around me.*
> *In beauty it is finished.*

Enjoy, remember always, and share the *Harmony* and *Balance* in *The Navajo Brothers and the Stolen Herd* with others.

Jack Rushing
(Lo La Ma)

ACKNOWLEDGMENTS

I am greatly indebted to the following for their help in producing this book: Dr. Laurence C. and Maurine Smith for their editorial assistance, encouragement, and many conversations throughout the writing project.

My brother, C. W. Parker, Missouri educator, former mayor of Waynesville, Missouri, writer, public speaker; he took a scholar's approach to seeing that the story was told in the best way possible.

Sidney J. Thomas, Jr., retired administrative assistant from Sandia National Laboratories, whose lifelong interest in Indians was derived from both parents. His father was a Smithsonian anthropologist, and his mother was a teacher on the Navajo Reservation.

Chenoa Bah Stilwell, Miss Indian U.S.A., 1990–1991, for Navajo translations. She began her internship at the White House in President Bush's Thousand Points of Light program in January 1992.

Many others have helped by reading the manuscript or assisted with details: Charlotte Bloom; Wilson Guerrero, a Navajo Indian from the Alamo Reservation; Katherine McMahon; Lucille Mulcahy; and Col. (Ret.) Joseph and Jean Holcombe.

My special thanks to Cathy Harper for assistance with the many details in manuscript preparation and correspondence, and to Dennis Dutton for editing the book.

THE NAVAJO BROTHERS ▲ AND ▼ THE STOLEN HERD

ROBBERS

All day Chee and Pahee had crept up the steep slope. They were Navajos, and knew how to hide. The sagebrush and beargrass concealed them if they crawled flat on the dry, rocky earth, but that was getting painful. The autumn sun burned through the jackets of the two brothers, and their knees and elbows were raw from contact with the rough ground, but they kept on. They could still see their flock of sheep in the valley far below and the strange men driving it, two on horseback wearing pistols, one walking alongside a packhorse.

"They are robbing our sheep!" said Chee, the oldest, in low, angry tones. "Our family's sheep!" His face wrinkled with misery. Pahee nodded excitedly, panting in fatigue.

"We must keep the thieves in sight," he went on. "We can rest among the cedars at the top of the ridge. They will make camp before dark. Maybe at the first water hole."

"Can we not return home for our father?" asked Pahee.

"I do not think so," replied Chee. "We must keep the herd in sight."

The two boys crouched low, making their way from clump to clump, reaching the top of the range an hour before sunset. They stood up among the dwarf cedars and watched.

They could see the men urging the sheep on. Every step carried the flock farther from their grazing ground. Already they were miles off their range. The boys looked at each other helplessly, with eyes both fearful and angry.

Chee and Pahee had cared for their family's flocks—which always included a few goats among the sheep—since they were old enough to tramp along after the stragglers and build their own shelter high in the mountains of the summer range. They knew the habits of their flocks as well as those of the wild animals of the southern Rockies. The three thieves could not be dealt with by the simple means their father used against coyotes, bobcats, mountain lions, and bears, for neither Pahee nor Chee carried weapons with them.

Without words, the two brothers watched the long line of sheep, nearly one hundred of them, round up at a clear spot far down the slope to the east, where there was apparently a water hole. They saw two of the robbers walking round the flock to quiet them for the night. The other gathered sticks and brush, and soon the smoke of his fire floated low and mingled with the darkening shadows of sunset.

With darkness came new courage to Chee and Pahee. They took in every movement of the men below. The two men who had walked around the flock now returned to the fire, one of them pulling a struggling sheep along with a rope and the other pushing from behind. The men looked comical, but Pahee and Chee could not laugh as they watched the third man quickly slaughter and butcher the sheep. Soon the three were feasting on roasted mutton.

"They eat meat that is not their own," said Pahee, looking at Chee.

"They shall not rob us of our family's sheep," said Chee. "We must take our flock back to our own range," he continued fiercely. "We shall punish the men who drive away our animals while we must hide like foxes to save our lives."

Pahee and Chee had been away from their hogan since early spring. Now it was near the time for the first frost, when they must soon start on their journey home.

Chee knelt and, stretching his lean legs on the still warm earth, lay down on his side, a bent arm supporting his weary head as he watched the scene below. Pahee also knelt, sitting beside his elder brother. Not a word was spoken for some time. The bleating of the sheep had stopped. The campfire far below was a red glow now, with an occasional flare of flame that showed three dark figures lying near it.

"Let us drive the herd away while the lazy robbers sleep," said Pahee.

Chee looked at his younger brother in surprise.

"I know we can't do that," Pahee apologized. "They might shoot us. But we must somehow get our sheep."

After several moments, Chee spoke. "The men must be from the Ladron Mountains to the east. They will drive the sheep there. Once in the malpais and arroyos of the Ladron slopes, a herd of sheep even twice as big as ours would never be found. There, I have heard, lazy thieves hide and eat till summer comes again. Then herds disappear just as ours is disappearing. We are perched above those thieves like eagles," he mused, "and yet we are helpless."

Chee's muscular frame jerked with emotion as he sat erect. He was a strong boy and sixteen, but the strain of the day had been hard, almost unbearable.

"Eagles watch from high places, then fly quickly upon their prey and are off," said Pahee as if to comfort his brother. "We'll keep watching. Our chance will come."

"Pahee," said Chee with a penetrating look at his brother, "you are two years younger than I, but you were born older."

Pahee swelled with pride and held back the remark he meant to make about being hungry and thirsty. "We'll follow them. Our chance must come," he said instead.

The quiet that settled on the ridge was so deep that Pahee's breathing kept Chee wide awake and alert. The small night animals whisking about made soft swishes in nearby bunches of saltgrass or light crackles in the dry sagebrush. Kangaroo rats in search of piñon cones jumped clumsily about the trees near Chee, revealing flashes of white bellies that identified them in the darkness. In the wild stillness, Chee thought manfully while Pahee slept.

At last a black darkness in the eastern horizon told Chee that morning was a few hours off, and he curled himself against his brother. He had decided what they must do to gain back their flock.

In the branches of a dead cedar a mountain owl chattered. Pahee moved closer to Chee. "Witches in these strange mountains laugh at us," he whispered. Chee made no comment.

Tired as the two young shepherds were, and as accustomed to mountain beds under the skies as they had been from babyhood, their sleep was still far from sound.

Since early morning they had had no food. They had seen the three men riding around their herd just as they sat at breakfast in their summer shelter about fifty feet up a mountain among the thick sagebrush. They had instinctively covered their little fire with dirt on seeing strangers, and had flattened themselves from sight. The boys had made out that the two men on horses were white, *billa'aga'na*. The other might be an Indian, but he did not look Navajo. Chee had whispered "*ches chilly* (curly hair)!" as he called Pahee's attention to the light, curly hair of the man on the roan bronco that passed not fifty feet from their hiding place. The two shepherds were enjoying their situation and the advantage they had over the men, who were probably only looking for bears or mountain lions. Or they might be sheep buyers; but the Navajo boys had none to sell, so why show themselves?

It was not till the three strange men were actually rounding up the flock and moving them toward the east that Chee and Pahee knew they were thieves. They had heard an occasional tale of a flock that disappeared completely when herders had gone for provisions or to a feast at some far-off place. Now their own flock, all the sheep their parents owned, was being driven away before their eyes. And they, their parents' trusted shepherds, were hiding in the sagebrush!

All that day, as the two young Indian boys had crept from one hiding place to another, leaving most of their few supplies behind them to make traveling easier, they had kept the moving flock and the drivers in sight. All day, the two had tried to think of a plan to rescue their sheep from the three men they now knew were bad, and probably dangerous. They knew such men gathered in small groups in the rugged, lava-split mesas and slopes of the Ladron Mountains. The wild nature of the Ladron country, except for trails known to the inhabitants alone, made it a safe retreat, where thieves and rustlers could be safe among their kind.

Chee had recalled, as they crept to the top of the ridge at sunset, how his grandfather and an uncle had hunted once in the wild country of the Ladrons and had come upon a robbers' camp, only recently abandoned. Once he had seen a picture of what his uncle said was the place.

The chill of this first night high in the mountains made sleeping without blankets uncomfortable, and Chee opened his eyes just as the top of the range to the east began to redden. Pahee shivered beside him, his eyes wide open. There was yet no stir to be seen at the camp below.

"The thieves will be moving again when the sun has warmed their backs and their wicked bellies are full of dishonest mutton," said Chee. "I must get among them somehow, to spy upon them and gather information. You stay hidden nearby. Signal me with smoke where you are from time to time. Can you do this?"

"Yes," said Pahee with determination.

"In the dark when you hear the chatter of the crazy owl, listen for the whistling chirp of the rock wren. Three times you will hear the chirp, and afterward you will answer with the call of the piñon jay. I will then come to you." On hearing the plan, Pahee sat up suddenly.

"I can do it, my brother. But if you do get into the robbers' camp you could be killed!"

"I'd rather lose my life than fail in our parents' trust," said Chee calmly.

"I am as brave as you," answered Pahee earnestly.

"Then follow my orders."

"That I will do," promised Pahee with an admiring look at his brother.

"I could trust no other as I can you, *yazzhie* (little one)," Chee replied, with a brown hand laid tenderly on Pahee's glossy black head.

"I need an hour start on them," he went on. "I can skirt the valley over there and meet them in the gap straight to the east. Coming from that direction, the thieves will not suspect I belong with the stolen flock."

"But the sheep will!" exclaimed Pahee. "Old Tlee Zee (Big Horns) will run to you as if you were his mother. The others will follow and mill about you, bleating."

"The sheep will be glad," answered Chee, with a smile. "They are as unhappy being led away from their owners as we are following helplessly after them. You keep the robbers in sight during the day. Get as near the camp as you can, safely, at night. Signal with the smoke at sunset, just for a moment. You have matches?" asked Chee.

"Enough for a few days," answered Pahee. "I will use flint if I run out."

"Good. Then listen in the night for my call."

With a quick pat on Pahee's shoulder, Chee slipped away and was soon far down among the dwarf cedar, mesquite, and greasewood that grew thick at the base of the mountain range.

Pahee suddenly felt a terrible loneliness, but bravely tried to turn his thoughts to the job ahead. It would be easier, he thought, to race his way along, skirting the edges of canyons close enough to have smoother travel, yet far enough up to take advantage of the concealing thickets. He imagined Chee speeding along—already on his way to some spot far ahead where the herd would later arrive. Then Pahee thought of his father and mother, of their hogan so many miles away among the greasewood—and near a spring. His mouth was dry, and he was thirsty, but the thought of the spring from which his mother carried water somehow comforted him. He thought of his baby sister and closed his eyes to hold back tears. She would be wide awake by now, her big dark eyes blinking in the sun as she leaned against the logs of the hogan. Bound securely in her cradle of strong wood, and laced in tightly with buckskin strips, the little one was safe and happy. For hours she would lean against a rock or the wall of the hogan, or swing clumsily from the low branches of a piñon tree or dwarf cedar. His mother would be at the loom. Pahee saw every detail.

Pahee rose and stretched his stiffened legs. He must find his own breakfast. The berries that grew near him only made hunger worse. He would have none of them. Just across a little gulch to his left he could see the huge sprout of a plant among several full-grown ones. He made his way there in a few seconds, broke down the sprout and peeled it as he ate. Cooked in hot stones, this starchy

sprout was delicious. Pahee knew just how to prepare it, but he had no intention of revealing his location by the smoke of even the smallest fire. The robbers, he thought as he ate, would keep a watch behind them. In front of them, however, they would sense no danger from the owners of the flock. Chee was clever with his plan. Pahee grinned savagely, thinking of this as he made his way to a lookout on the ridge.

The sun was an hour high when the three men below finally saddled their horses, loaded the packhorse, and started the unwilling herd ahead. Pahee could distinguish a few familiar animals. He saw the goat Tlee Zee breaking his way back among the bleating sheep as if to lead them in open revolt against their captors and return again to familiar range. He could see a rider, the man with curly hair, bang a knotted rope into the old goat's face, and after much effort turn its head toward the east again. The goat with the big curled horns had long been the leader, and the inside guard of the flock. He was aggressive toward strangers, but to Pahee and Chee was always gentle as a ewe.

Pahee watched the robbers leave. As soon as he dared, he followed. Keeping well concealed, he soon reached their abandoned camp. The campfire was dying to white ashes. Nothing remained that a boy could eat. A tin can lay in the ashes. Pahee grabbed it up. It was empty, but the half-charred label pictured a dish of brown beans striped with crispy, curling bacon. Despite his thirst, Pahee's mouth watered at the sight. He decided he would carry the can and fill it with water at the first creek or water hole. He was just turning to slip back into the thicket when he spied the skins of some baked potatoes in the ashes of the fire. He was tempted to eat them, but instead stuffed them in his jacket and went as quickly as safety would allow to the water hole where the herd had drunk. Here Pahee drank his fill. He drank till the water ran from his mouth and nose. Finally he could hold no more. The thought grieved him some, but he filled his can carefully and started off to gain the elevation that gave him the advantage he must keep and the concealment he needed.

The going would not be so hard in the morning, but the boy dreaded the noonday. Beating down as he knew it would in a few hours, the hot sun would bring thirst, and hunger would come again soon. Pahee thought about the potato skins as he went, and stopped every now and then to lap delightedly with his tongue at the edge of the can. This can might keep him from too great a thirst until he could reach another spring, mountain creek, or water hole. He thought of Chee many times and wished that his brother had the water and potato skins he carried. He would try to save them for a feast when Chee came to him that night. Then they would eat and drink together.

TWO

WAITING

Meanwhile, Chee, hurrying far ahead, strained every nerve to reach the gap through which the herd must pass. Midday found him in clearer country, but without a trail of any kind. From a height he would get his bearing, sight the gap, and plunge again in the direction he must go.

As he neared the gap that formed the pass through the mountain range, Chee found the country more level but so broken by ancient lava flows, dry creek beds, and rocky arroyos that he was near exhaustion before he reached the gap. He had not allowed himself to think of food, but water he must have soon. He rested for a few minutes in the shadow of the peak he had left behind. The rest did nothing to relieve his thirst, but it gave him renewed energy with which to find a way to quench the thirst that could not be endured much longer. What good could come of his dying from thirst? He would rather the thieves kill him in a fight for his family's sheep. There was no reason to throw away his life uselessly. No. He would make for the lowest country, find water and be stronger for the time when he should meet the rustlers. But Pahee? The thought that his younger brother might be suffering as he was angered him suddenly.

Chee calmed his anger, however, and forced himself on, downward and toward the peaks that marked the gap. In the dry bed of a gully he was following, he finally noticed a spot ahead where moist sand had been dug. He ran to the spot. Around it he found the tracks of a coyote. The coyote had dug. Now Chee dug. His hands tore deep into the gravelly soil that all but dripped with moisture, but gave none to drink as yet. He rested, then dug again. At last, the hole, quite wide and deep now, began to show little trickles of water. How slowly it came. The boy buried his face in the wet gravel to cool off, then drew his head up again to peer—half fearfully—into the hole. Yes, water was coming. He dug a large enough opening to admit his head and shoulders. Then he thought of Pahee—and suddenly he had a notion not to drink. Maybe his little brother was also crazed from thirst. Maybe the thieves had taken him slave as the Spaniards had done with some of the *Dinè* (Navajo) children years and years ago.

"Pahee will not throw away his life. He will exchange it bravely for what he can get." With this thought, Chee lowered his head and shoulders into the hole. He drank as moderately as he could, raising his head from time to time, only to sink it out of sight again.

The sun was nearing the top of the mountain range behind him. Chee thought of Pahee again, and hurried on toward the gap, reaching the pass an hour or more before sunset. Here he found a high point and flung himself down to watch for the coming of the flock. He was not tired now, nor thirsty. A few green fruits of the yucca with berries and buds that he had gathered on the way eased his hunger some. He could also, perhaps, find a rock squirrel, or a rabbit. No. He would watch for the coming of the herd. They would reach the gap by sunset and make camp. Pahee would signal his whereabouts, and Chee would join him in the night to make plans. Chee tried to doze, knowing he needed strength that sleep would give, but his eyes would scarcely close before he would rise again and scan the country to the west. Still no flock appeared. At last, the sun slipped out of sight behind the farthest mountains.

Chee stood and scanned the rough country over which he had made his way. Still no herd nor drivers. Could they have taken a sharp turn to the south? There was no pass through the spur that shut off that direction completely with its tall, wall-like ridge that ran for miles.

Then, miles back along the very brakes he had crossed early after midday, but higher up the slope, Chee saw a single column of pale, whitish smoke. The robbers, or Pahee? His heart pounded. Then another column perhaps a quarter mile from the first. It rose straight and white high above the trees, and then soon melted away into nothingness. Pahee. Chee hoped the rustlers would not see his signal.

He lowered himself to the ground with a sudden weariness and relief. Pahee was, as yet, safe and well. But why had not the drivers kept on? Why camp with just half the expected distance covered? It would be impossible now to reach Pahee's hiding place and return to his own by daylight. His legs were perhaps not too tired, but his moccasins showed the scars of heavy wear. Another trip across the sharp volcanic rocks of the malpais and back would make him barefooted. Besides, he must have some rest for his body, and a little time to think. After standing to take another look in the direction of where his brother's signal had come from, Chee dropped to the prickly ground and quickly fell asleep.

Meanwhile, Pahee had killed a rabbit with a throwing stick he had whittled and was roasting it over coals of charred wood. Charred wood fire made good heat, and was easily hidden—no blaze to flare up and show the camper sitting beside it and reveal his hiding place to his enemies, camped so close below and to the east. He had watched them make camp at midafternoon and wondered why they had not driven on till night stopped them. The two white men had sat near each other on the ground all the afternoon. The Indian seemed to have the care of the flock tonight, for Pahee had seen him quiet the sheep at sundown. He then brought to the campfire a keg of water from a small mountain stream and unloaded the packhorse. The horses, freed of their saddles and their front feet fastened together, ate the prickly grass and weeds, nibbling now and then at a more tender twig of sage or greasewood.

Pahee sat quietly beside his tiny fire. On the ground near his elbow was spread a royal feast—roast rabbit, baked potato skins, and a can partly full of water. Try as he might, he had not been able to carry the can without spilling some water from time to time. Still, there was enough left for a good taste or two for Chee when he came. Pahee had also seen the Indian carry the keg, and knew the direction to water. He would slip down into the flock a few hours before dawn and fill his can with milk from a goat or sheep for the next day's travel.

Time moved slowly for Pahee as he listened high among the cedars and shrubs on the mountainside. He dared not close his eyes, for his ears, dulled with sleep, might then miss the call he listened for.

The moon rose only a few feet above the eastern horizon, and seemed to sink again as suddenly as it had appeared. Pahee knew it was long past midnight, and he was worried for Chee. The heavy darkness that precedes dawn in the mountains—and the cold—settled down on the lone boy. Then at last he rose, finished the water he had saved for his brother, and made his way down the slope. The whitened trunk of a dead cedar near his small camp held its crooked limbs out like skeleton arms. This foreboding sight would help him find his way back in a few minutes. It would be an empty camp; Chee would not come to him at this hour.

Pahee had wished for his dog during the night, but was glad that the robbers had none. "I would not be the dog of a thief," he said to himself as he slipped quietly among the animals at the edge of the flock. Two she-goats jumped to their feet in an instant, recognizing him, and set their legs wide, offering their milk. Pahee could have thrown his arms about them and cried for joy, he was so lonesome, but he only patted them and drew their milk as fast as he could. He filled the can and gulped the warm milk, then filled it again. He patted the animals near him once more, and then quickly slipped away in the direction from which he had come.

By the time Pahee reached the slope that held his camp, the darkness was greying a little in the east. From a distance, he could still make out the scrawny, gnarled limbs of the dead tree by his camp and, indistinct as they were, they guided him to the spot where he had left the untouched supper.

But the supper was gone! Not a morsel remained as far as Pahee could see by the half-darkness. Could Chee have come while he was away? But then, what could have made him leave so soon? His heart almost stopped. His head felt queer. As soon as he could trust his breath, Pahee ventured the call of the piñon jay. Again he called—and listened. No, Chee must not have been to the camp.

The boy sat down on a crooked root of the skeleton tree and waited. In his hands he clutched the can of milk, which warmed his hands as it did his belly. The sky reddened. It seemed to bring even more warmth with its color. Pahee examined his camp. Of the supper, not even a shred of potato skin was left. Where the little fire had been, the boy saw animal signs, and dog-like tracks indicating the owner had kicked dirt and twigs scornfully behind him before leaving the defiled spot.

"*Chinde!*" exclaimed Pahee. "The son of a devil coyote!" Then, in quieter tones: "Must there be thieves, too, even among wild animals?"

The warm milk that the boy had drunk made him feel drowsy despite his anger over losing his food, and he leaned against the trunk of the dead cedar and dozed with half-open eyes. He could soon see the robbers below, for the sun was not far behind the top of the high peaks to the east. Pahee grew determined. He would be ready to follow them when they started the herd ahead.

The sun was two hours up when the thieves finally broke camp. Pahee had watched every move. He hated to see an Indian with such men. That the Indian was not of his tribe he well knew now, for the man did not dress or move like one of the *Dinè*. Yet, why should this man, who was still, after all, an Indian, choose white companions such as these? Did he live in Ladron Mountains to hide his bad deeds as white men did? Pahee repeated: "Not Navajo, but I am still for some reason afraid for him."

Pahee rested at his lookout for an hour after the men had gone. He could see a cloud of yellowish dust far down the narrow valley and knew the sheep were moving at a fair pace. The morning was cool, with a fresh breeze blowing from the east, but not as cold as before. The going would be easier now that he need not hide, now that he was going to put his plan into effect. It was even rather pleasant. He took off his moccasins. They were wearing badly. He could walk easily without them in the daylight. With rawhide string he tied them together, and threw them about his neck; he went on with a lightness in his heart that he felt, but did not understand.

THREE

A "TREED"
INJUN

The sun was straight overhead by the time
the robbers reached the narrow pass in the mountains.
They halted for a hurried meal. Pahee kept as close as he
dared. He drank the last of the milk and stuffed the empty
can into his jacket. There was some commotion among the
flock in front. The goats had bunched under a tree where
the sheep crowded about them. The curly-haired robber
rode ahead to locate the trouble. He soon returned with a
rider behind his saddle.

"A 'treed' Injun as I live!" he said, laughing as he threw
himself from the roan horse. "The sheep had him scared
that bad he could have clumb a greased pole. Git off, Injun.
The lambs won't eat you."

Pahee had seen the robber return with Chee. So this
was Chee's plan—to get caught in order to spy upon the
rustlers' camp! Pahee was terrified, yet so proud of his
brother's courage that he feared the beating of his heart
might attract the thieves and undo all that Chee had
accomplished.

It took much motioning and explaining, apparently, to
make Chee understand that the white men were urging
him to get off the horse and join them at lunch. He pre-

tended fright at even the bleating of a lamb, and made as if to mount the horse again. The men laughed so boisterously that Pahee could hear their laughter clearly. He wished he could also hear them talking.

"Something wrong with an Injun that's afraid of sheep," said the dark man. "I've heard they even eat 'em raw." He grinned crookedly, showing an ugly purplish scar at the corner of his mouth.

"Is that so, Redskin?" asked the curly-haired one. Chee made no sign of understanding.

"You talk to him, Yaqui," he said, addressing their Indian. "Maybe that lingo of yours might click."

The strange Indian spoke in guttural syllables and husky cheek sounds. It seemed to make no impression on Chee.

"He not Yaqui," said the Indian.

As the men ate, Chee gnawed hungrily on a dry biscuit, shaking his head at the mutton they pressed upon him. He listened with all his might. The white men spoke good English. The Yaqui seemed to understand it fairly well, but spoke it very little. The man Chee and Pahee had called Ches Chilly really did seem to be named "Curly." The swarthy one addressed as "Claw" had black, mole-like eyes, a scar across his cheek, a hand from which all parts save the thumb and forefinger were gone, and a crooked— very crooked—grin. The other thief was an Indian, probably from Mexico as he answered to the name "Yaqui."

Chee took in all he could hear and see, but showed no concern. He seemed unable to understand much, even when motions were elaborately substituted for words.

"We've got a dumb one now," said Curly, "barely knows enough to feed himself, judgin' from the way he turned down the mutton for the cold dough-bullets Claw calls biscuits."

"If some folks are so smart, looks like they'd make the dough-bullets for once," sneered Claw.

Curly and Yaqui laughed. Claw seemed to enjoy the ribaldry but made little show of merriment. Chee kept his face blank.

During the meal Pahee had watched every move. He could hear little of the conversation, only that which the wind brought him from time to time, but that took away none of his interest nor his caution. From his hiding place he watched the men round up the flock after their meal and start ahead. Chee was riding on the roan behind Curly, with Yaqui leading the packhorse.

Pahee followed his brother with eyes shining with pride. As the last rider rounded the point that guarded the south entrance to the pass, then turned toward the south and disappeared in the dust-cloud raised by the sheep, the boy hung his moccasins lightly across his shoulders and was off with renewed spirit. There was no doubt now that the thieves were making for their rendezvous among the Ladron Mountains.

Water was not plentiful, but a creek choked with boulders from the slopes wound its way through the gap and provided a thin stream. Pahee drank often of the icy water and felt less hunger than on the day before, though he occasionally cursed the coyote who had stolen his feast. "*Chinde!*" he would say at times. "The son of a devil coyote!

A thief among the wild animals!" Sometimes the boy would smile in spite of his hunger as he thought of the trick the coyote had played on him. Sometimes he even imagined the sly animal peeping from some bush and holding his sides at Pahee's surprise on finding the feast gone. At these thoughts the boy laughed too, the low, gentle laugh of the Navajo.

Toward midafternoon Pahee drew so near the drivers that he had to keep well among the feathery mesquite and greasewood. Forgetting for a moment—even for a single step—and exposing himself to the keen eyes of the robbers would spoil whatever plans Chee had made. It would, doubtless, also cost his brother's life.

Reaching an open, gravelly park where rockslides had sheared the slope of vegetation, Pahee crept into the little creek and made his way among the boulders of its bed. He had cautiously fallen back. He could take no risk of disclosing to the drivers that they were being followed. They would kill him. Of this he had no doubt. And Chee was with them!

The mountains far to the west were high. The sun went down behind them at last, and a long twilight followed. Pahee made his way to higher ground directly north of the herd, now halted for the night. He watched the men making camp. He could see Chee caring for the horses. The Indian was unloading the packhorse. The two others walked about the tired flock, bunching them into a smaller area where they would soon lie down. Pahee saw the two look in his direction twice. The dark one motioned toward the very slope on which he lay. Surely he had not been seen!

His breath quickened. Then he moved farther up where greasewood, sagebrush, and Spanish bayonet grew thorny and thick. He shifted to a more inaccessible point farther east. The sun was down. Soon his signal must rise. Chee would be watching. It would, perhaps, be impossible for him to slip away, but he would know his younger brother had not failed him.

Two flinty stones, knocked raspingly together in rapid succession, threw a thin line of sparks into the dry, shredded bark Pahee had placed in a groove between two rocks. He had run out of matches, but he knew how to make do without them. A spark caught, and the boy blew his breath gently upon it. Rotted pieces of dry cedar placed on the slowly burning bark soon became red coals. They would hold the fire. At the right time, Pahee had a tiny bluish column of smoke rising into the air high up the mountain. Pahee kept the smoldering fire small, but sufficient to provide just the volume of smoke he needed. He knew Chee could detect the small cloud it made in the sky, should he miss the rising column itself. But soon he had to bank the fire or risk discovery by the rustlers. He hoped Chee had seen it.

Darkness came quickly once the sun had set over the last range to the west. The camp below was quiet in an hour or two. Pahee built a fire in a hole under a rock. The hole faced the north, so not even a glow, he hoped, could be seen from the south. The boy laid green fruits of the yucca, the tips of several woody shoots of a tall plant, and two Indian potatoes he had dug early in the day into the coals. He would feast tonight, and no *chinde* coyote would spoil his feast. He could not expect his brother to slip away from the robbers yet, as he would be watched too closely for a while.

Pahee fished bits of food from his fire as the night grew on. The woody shoots were really delicious once the starchy pith inside was cooked. The green fruit of the yucca was a little bitter, but the pulp inside was pleasant to the taste. The Indian potato was a delicacy he devoured entirely. Pahee and Chee had always saved the wild potato for the very last. With wild garlic and mutton, the Indian potato was food for a chief. Pahee dozed as he thought of such a feast.

Several hours later, the boy was brought to his senses by the chattering of an owl in a tree apparently not far up the slope. Again the crazy chatter. Pahee held his breath so not to miss a sound. Then—yes!—it was the whistling chirp of the rock-wren! Three times it sang, then there was silence. Pahee sprang to his feet. He dared not trust his voice, so he whispered the call of the piñon jay. Encouraged by the imitation, he called again, this time more loudly. The answer came, not more than a few feet away, and then Chee bounded into Pahee's camp!

"A moon since I saw you, little brother!" he whispered as he threw himself on the ground and clasped his arms around Pahee's knees.

"And you are unhurt. I am very happy, my brother," answered Pahee, kneeling and clasping his brother's shoulders. "I have been glad to see you down there and know you are safe. If, like an eagle, I have watched our sheep by day from far above, I have, like a bobcat, been among them in the night."

Here Pahee, with some elaboration, offered his visitor the can of milk. "It is not long from the goat," he explained. "I have not heated it. But coals are plenty in my fireplace."

Pahee could not see the pride and admiration in the face of his brother, but raked a few coals from the ashes and piled bits of charred sticks upon them. "Our mother heats the milk hot," he said, carefully setting the can on the little fire.

"Yes," answered Chee, following Pahee's example and curling low beside the fire. "I knew you would be somewhere near," he went on, "but dared not look too carefully or long. But the men down there seem not to watch. They look without seeing," he added softly. "Except for the Indian, perhaps. I do not know about him."

"What do they think about you, I wonder?" ventured Pahee.

"So far, I don't know," Chee replied, "but they are sure I am a stranger to the sheep. They think I am afraid of them!" Both boys laughed softly.

"When the flock met me at the gap, Old Tlee Zee brought the leaders straight to me on a run. I climbed the tree that stood near. You would have pitied the old ram-goat if you had seen how strange his big brown eyes were when he looked up at me and I said no friendly word. The sheep, too. The old ewe whose broken leg we tied with flat sticks had been the first to come. One of the herders called Ches Chilly (the others call him Curly) saw the herd bunching under the tree and came. I yelled as if scared of the goats and sheep, and made motions to be saved from them. He talks good English. He laughed at me and told me the sheep wouldn't eat me. I pretended not to understand, but made as if crying and talked fast in Navajo, saying

Dichin nisin! Shímá sání bidisilíí!
Chee Mal Yazzie nisin! Chee Mal Yazzie!

I'm hungry! I'm lonesome for my Grandmother!
I want Chee Mal Yazzie! Chee Mal Yazzie!

" 'Come on down, you fool,' the man said, 'and stop yelling,' but I kept on crying louder and louder. Then he drove off the flock and motioned me to get on behind the saddle. I dropped from my limb to the roan horse, trembling and shaking. The man laughed and started to trot. I made like falling off, but held on to the man's waist.

"This robber had two guns on a strap and a double belt of cartridges. He looks young and not unkind, but his pale blue eyes are wicked even when he laughs. He is younger than the other white man, the one they call 'Claw,' whose left hand is like an owl's foot, with but a thumb and one finger. He is dark, and a crooked scar from his mouth to one ear makes his laugh go to the ugly side. But he laughs little. He is a man with no kindness in his eyes.

"The other thief is an Indian, maybe a Yaqui. That's what they call him. Speaks poor English and only answers the things the others ask. He looks at me much when the others don't see. I speak no English word to any of them and make like I don't seem to understand when they talk, even to me. Yesterday Claw asked Curly if he thought me a runaway from the mines in Mexico as Yaqui was. 'Might be,' he said. 'These Injuns drift from one place to another.

Home's where their hat's off.' Then he looked at me.

" 'Where's your hat, Redskin?' he asked. I only shook my head, pretending not to understand.

" 'Well, since his hat's off, he must be at home then, according to you,' Claw said. 'After all, maybe that's why so many Injuns don't wear hats. They're wild, they're at home anywhere. Even Yaqui here, that thing he wears couldn't be called a hat!' Yaqui wears a ragged sombrero made of yucca."

"They are going to the Ladrones?" asked Pahee.

"They are on their way," sighed Chee. "Another good day's drive will bring them to the open mesa and valley between high mountains. There they plan to camp for some days—a week or two, might be. They say there is good feed there and nobody knows the place."

Chee looked at the night sky. He pointed. "The moon will be up soon. When it goes down I must go back. Because I am afraid of the sheep and goats, they put me to stay near the horses. They are hobbled, only a little way down from here. The hobbles are held fast to the front feet with a padlock. Only Claw has a key."

The two brothers sipped the hot milk leisurely. Chee drew a large, flinty biscuit from his blouse. "Claw makes them," he said. "I brought it to you. When Claw saw me gnaw it, he grinned a little. I looked toward the mountain. I don't like to see him laugh, even a little. The blue scar on his face!"

Pahee broke the biscuit.

"You eat it all," Chee said, pushing aside the proffered portion. "I have a better chance to eat than you, even if only beans and biscuits. They have mutton at every meal, and Yaqui cooks it well—cooks it just as mother says Uncle Yazzhie used to—but I pretend to be unwilling to eat of animals strange to me. Our family's own mutton! They killed the brown ewe our mother has kept so long for color in her rugs!"

The boys were thoughtful for a moment. "With you on the outside and me with the rustlers, we will be able to take advantage of any chance that comes," Chee said.

"Sometimes I feel that Yaqui, too, is waiting for a chance," he added. "When the two white men are playing cards in the camp, Yaqui sits braiding horsehair ornaments. That is why the horses have short tails and scant manes." Both boys laughed quietly. "His bridle is made of horsehair, even the reins. He wears a belt, but carries no gun. Claw has one pistol like Curly's. Another very small one he carries in a pocket under his arm. It is not like a common pistol, but I'm sure it is a gun. We must be careful," Chee added. "The men carry these guns to kill. We can only wait. Every hour I am in the robbers' camp I shall listen, and think."

The boys sat silent for several moments, looking at the small fire and thinking their own thoughts. Then Chee said:

*Nítch'i Diyinii ndédidiłkił dził diyinii biło
ha'a'aahdę́ę́' Sisnaajiní, shádi'aahdę́ę́' Tsoodził,
e'e'aahdę́ę́' Dook'o'oosłííd, náhookǫsdę́ę́' Dibé Nstaa,
dibé Shindadiłtééł doo niha'a'yádó diné doo
yá'áshxóonii, tádidíín benadandon'í.*

We will ask the spirits of the East of Sierra Blanca Peak, the South of Mt. Taylor Peak, the West of San Francisco Peak, and the North of La Plata Mountain to help us get our sheep back and protect us from these evil men. We will make an offering of corn pollen.

With that, Chee drew a small buckskin bag from a string on his neck. Both boys then stood as the elder one took some of the sacred meal and gourd pollen from the bag, and tossed a tiny pinch to each of the four directions.

"I have made prayer plumes, and placed them among rocks all along the way," said Pahee earnestly, "and to-night when I went for the milk, I buried owl feathers as near the wicked men as I could for their bad luck. Tomorrow I will lag behind and sing a medicine song for our protection. I know the one that Hatali sang when his son went with his white friends to the white man's war across the sea. I shall sing it for you, my brother. It will keep you safe. Hatali's son returned to his land though many others were never seen again."

"I, too, know the song, Pahee," said Chee, "and have whispered it for you many times today."

Together they sang quietly:

Nííłch'í Diyinii 'alííli oee nhich'ą́ą́h na'adá
nhika'adiłwoł,
Shidą́ą́hdę́ę́',
nishł'ádę́ę́',
nish'náádę́ę́'
'akéshdę́ę́'

Shikékłáádéé̜',
Shitsiitahdéé̜',
T'áá 'ałtsogo hó̜zhó̜ docłeeł

Great Spirit Protection,
Please help me in front,
And both my sides,
And the back of me,
And under me,
And on top of me;
Be well,
Everything be well!

The moon had gone. The few stars were dim. The heavy darkness that comes an hour or two before day gathered thickly upon the horizon. Then Chee slipped stealthily down the slope to the horses, now lying with noses resting heavily on the ground. Only the packhorse raised his head. Chee crept near and lay down.

FOUR

THE
DUTCHMAN'S
STORE

As far as the flock was concerned it now mattered little where they went. Navajo sheep are accustomed to new surroundings during the months from early spring to late fall. The young herders drive them high into the mountains as soon as the snow on the slopes begins to melt, not to return to winter feeding grounds in the lowlands till driven down by early winter storms. Chee and Pahee saw their sheep enjoying the uncropped range that furnished more abundant pasture each day, and noted the gain the animals were making on full rations of grass and water. Could they have been sure of the flock's return, the two boys would gladly have followed far south to the strange low range where it was said no sheep had ever grazed. But their herd was in the possession of ruthless men who would have good food—their sheep!—when winter snows blocked mountain passes and made the dwellers within as safe as though in another world.

The sun had been up two hours before the herd began moving. The pasturage was rich and lovely. Chee let the packhorse walk lazily behind. If a sheep or goat started toward him, he quickly clambered aboard the packhorse, causing much laughter from the men, and many jibes throughout the day at his expense. He continued to refuse mutton, though his very soul threatened to cry out for some when he smelled it frying. But his visit to Pahee had so raised his spirits that he even sang as he plodded along in the afternoon. He had no fear now that his brother would lack for food. He would watch, listen, and plan, taking advantage of any opportunity presenting itself at any time. At supper that evening, Claw and Curly mentioned the stop they would make in three more days.

"Once on Gallina Mesa we might as well be on Mars," Curly had said with a satisfied chuckle. "The Dutchman ought to be stockin' up by now."

"Maybe," replied Claw. "Ought to ride down one of these days and look him over."

"It would be a pleasure to bump him off," said Curly with an unpleasant glitter in his pale blue eyes. "No man can keep the brand of tobacco he would carry and furnish it to me long."

"You out?" asked Claw.

"Only two packs left," Curly answered. "Creosote, moth balls and alfalfa hay—straight. Have one," he added with disgust, offering a cigarette to his companion. "In Chicago a guy that sells such tobacco would get the hot-seat."

"And the one that buys such . . . ," replied Claw, ". . . a hemp necktie?"

". . . ought to have a razor across his face," Curly answered, with an insolent look at Claw's scar.

Thrusting the package inside his jacket and producing a pack of oily cards, Curly began a game with Claw.

Chee had not understood all of the conversation. Some of the words puzzled him. The wary and angry way the two men had looked at each other as they talked made him uneasy. Yaqui sat not far off, busy with the brow-band for a bridle. His deft fingers wove the stiff, shiny hairs into a smooth, intricate design of brown and white. Chee cleaned up the supper things and laid the bedrolls out for Claw and Curly, then sat near Yaqui, intent upon learning his art. A casual glance as the sun went down satisfied the boy that his brother was less than a half mile to the north, and a bit east. The hobbled horses grazed halfway between them.

In spite of the relief his brother's signal brought, Chee suddenly felt lonely, terribly lonely. Even the sheep were beginning to lose interest in him. Only a few times during the day had a single one tried to renew old acquaintance, even then showing little curiosity at his changed behavior. That hurt him in a way he had never been hurt before. He would gladly have crept among the animals for the comfort they alone could offer in this wild spot where no trust could be placed in men—where even the two who seemed closest together somehow seemed more distrustful of each other than they were of strangers of a different race.

As darkness put an end to the game and to the braiding, the men prepared for bed. Only Yaqui removed any of his clothing. Curly and Claw slept as they were, fully dressed and armed. What could two men fear that fastened them to their weapons as securely as Claw locked the horses to their iron hobbles? Chee lay near the packhorse—thinking, hoping, waiting. Then, in the black darkness of late night, when he could hear the men breathing the slow breath of sleep, he slipped off to his brother. Returning shortly, but with renewed spirit, he crept near the resting horse and slept heavily.

In the few days that followed, Chee learned much. The conversations between Claw and Curly gradually clarified. Words and phrases in strange uses to him took on meaning, not always clear, to be sure, but sinister and revealing of the character and intentions of the two men. At meals, and at their games after supper, they paid little attention to Chee. Yaqui usually sat somewhat apart from the others, working industriously. Occasionally he lounged near the fire, singing low in a strange language that nobody seemed to regard as expressing any meaning. When Claw or Curly asked him the simplest common questions, he answered very poorly in their language but elaborated in his own, much to their amusement or to their disgust. Of Chee they asked little and seemed to expect less, making motions suffice almost entirely for speech.

"I don't believe the redskin can hear," Chee heard Curly say one day. "Might be a dummy playin' hooky from deaf school at Santa Fe. But that's pretty far from here."

"May be deaf, but an Injun can see—even deaf ones," said Claw. "Born trackers I've heard. Scent like a bloodhound. Follow a trail a week old."

"All bunk," said Curly, waving Claw's credulity aside with a gesture of finality. "Injuns are no different from whites—except duller, and can't carry as much firewater."

"I believe that gray stuff Yaqui chews keeps him dopey

most of the time. Harmless lookin' plant. Spreads out flat on the ground. You've heard of the wild tobacco," said Claw, "that the Injuns used to use?"

"They don't use it much now, it seems, not since Captain John Smith's time anyway," replied Curly with a grin. "But it couldn't be much worse than some tame varieties we've got now, like the Dutchman's."

Knowing how the two white men regarded him, Chee felt easier. He knew a Navajo boy who spent most of each year at the school for the deaf at Santa Fe. That boy used to make signs with his fingers. This gave Chee an idea. Why not be deaf, too, if the robbers thought him so?

"Better not do it," advised Pahee when Chee mentioned the idea to him that night. "They learn to read and write at that place. That boy we know can do both. The robbers would make you do that, and they might trick you into telling more than you want."

Chee looked with pride at Pahee—how intelligent he was!—and the two engaged in earnest conversation. Chee repeated in detail much that Claw and Curly had said. At last both boys agreed that Claw and Curly were not country people—that they were criminals from some northern city and hiding now among the mountains toward the Mexican border. Curly had once barely escaped hanging, and Claw's scar was from the slash of a razor, and the two were preparing for a siege in the mountains where they could remain hidden in safety with the sheep—for months if need be. In this preparation, they planned to kill a Dutchman at his trading store on the old trail to Silver City, rob him of his money and goods, and probably throw his body into an abandoned shaft or into a deep fissure in the lava. They would carry away what they wanted, and likely burn what was left. People coming to the trading store would think the trader had become discouraged and gone to another location. It would be months, maybe years, before the man would be missed or a search be made for him. The flock of sheep would provide fresh meat for the robbers' food supply till every one was eaten.

Chee told Pahee that though the white men were partners, he was sure they did not trust each other. In fact, he thought either one would gladly kill the other as soon as he could get along without him.

"In a day or two, Curly is going down to the trading store to look things over," Chee said as he left Pahee. "The place is west of here and south. From what they say it must be at the foot of the mountain with two peaks where the flatland slopes to the south. It is many miles from here by the creek trail, then over the mountain trail the San Carlos Apaches use on their way back from visits to the Mescaleros. But the trail is rough, and there is not much water."

"I can find that place!" said Pahee in excited whispers. "By daylight I can be well away from here. I'll keep to the Apache trail. I have followed parts of it already. It goes on west from here! In a few days I will be at the trading store. Say I may go, Chee," the boy said earnestly.

Chee drew a silver ring set with turquoise from a small buckskin bag under his belt. "Trade it for food and new shoes," he said as he offered it to Pahee. "See everything about the place; find out the direction to any settlement or town near it, and how far," he said.

"I have my own ring, and the heavy bracelet my father gave me," said Pahee, returning Chee's offer. "I will be glad to do something. Waiting idle like a brown hawk on the top of a dead cedar is harder than mountains or malpais. You can trust me. I will be glad to see Ches Chilly and the roan horse."

Chee laughed lightly, put his arms about the boy tenderly, and whispered, "Signal me when you return. I shall not sleep until I see you, my brother," he said, and crept down the gorge and out upon the sandy wash where the horses lay.

As soon as the first light began to show in the east, Pahee, with his tin can tucked into his shirt and his worn shoes now on his feet, made his way cautiously down the slope, out of the thickest of prickly vegetation and straight for the two-peaked mountain that marked the vicinity of the trader's store. When the sun was showing an edge over the tall range to the east, Pahee felt himself fairly safe. Not once in the days he had followed them had the robbers scouted their surroundings. They seemed well-acquainted with the lay of the country and trusted in the customary absence of even an occasional settler or lone prospector. They showed no fear of meeting an enemy, or of being overtaken from behind. They seemed to know that many flocks of sheep and goats roamed the mesas and slopes practically alone in summer, only to be rounded up in time to avoid the severe storms of late fall. Yet, these men were not natives of the country. Chee had said they were not even mountain men, but from the cities "far to the north of our border ranges," he recalled.

Coming upon the Apache trail, Pahee took off his shoes and again swung them upon his neck. He felt free and full of courage. He could run now, without fear of being seen. Trees grew tall on either side of the worn trail, rocky and washed by mountain cloudbursts. Along this route were wild grapes and bright berries. Mesquite pods full of succulent seeds were delicious eaten raw, and tender shoots and buds grew thick in the shade of taller trees. Nobody need go hungry on Apache trail. Water was not plentiful along the creek, to be sure, but Pahee knew somewhere this trail would pass a spring or bend down to touch a watering place at the creek.

Pahee thought of Chee's description of Curly: "Blue eyes—pale blue, maybe green." He repeated his brother's words, feeling sure he would recognize the man when he met him. The roan horse, too. He would know it half a mile away with its high, funny head and its short tail. Pahee laughed to himself and thought of the Yaqui. "Sometimes I wonder if he, too, is waiting for a chance," Chee had said.

In a few days, Pahee had reached a high mesa near the foot of the two-topped mountain. Climbing up its rather steep side to the high, level top, he could see for miles around. The lowland sloped rather abruptly to the south for some distance, then flattened into a gentler, more rolling plain. A few miles below him, in a green grotto of lava, was a lone settler. Pahee could make out what might be a dwelling, with two or three small out-buildings scattered among the trees that surrounded the house, save on the south. The tiny oasis in the lava gash must be the trader's, for not another dwelling was in sight. A few cattle and horses were grazing on the plain between him and the settler.

Pahee scrambled from his lookout and was soon on the easy way down. He had had little water during the day, but by the vegetation around the little settlement he knew there was a spring ahead. He had never seen country lying as this, falling away from the mountains in wide sheets of waste that seemed to slip on and on to the east and south, as far as he could see. The boy felt strange. He was awed by the comparatively level expanse of plain that slid away before him—treeless, arid, bare.

Going at a slower pace than he had gone on the mountain trail, Pahee found himself nearing the settlement by midafternoon. On a little rise a few dozen yards from the dwelling, the boy replaced his shoes. He looked anxiously at the new thin spots the early part of his journey had worn in sole and toe, and picked his way carefully. He neared a few grazing horses. They tossed their heads up, as one eyed him for an instant, then as suddenly threw their tails high and galloped away until they were a cloud of dust. If only Yaqui could have those tails!

Reaching the dwelling, Pahee made his way to the door, open except for a screen, and looked in.

"Come in, come in, young feller," said a big, cordial voice.

Pahee hesitated. A dog wagged his way to the screen lazily.

"Come in, young feller. Git out of the way, dog," said the voice as its owner appeared. "The old dog don't have many visitors, and he's mighty near as glad to see a customer as

I am," laughed the man, pushing the dog aside and opening the screen.

Pahee entered. He was dusty and dry. The trader was visiting with a Navajo man. The Navajo customer left, calling "*Ya-Te-yay*" to both of them.

"You must be thirsty comin' from most anywhere today," the trader said, pouring some water into a tin cup. He handed it to Pahee.

"Usually I'm here alone, but today Begay was helping me make a list of items his people will need this winter."

The boy drank greedily, and returned the empty tin with a "thank you" that made the man start.

"And you talk as good English as I can! Maybe better when you get goin', " he laughed. "Pull that stool up to the counter." Pahee obeyed.

"You've not been to dinner, have you?"

"I ate things along the way," he said. "I'm not very hungry. Up that way," said Pahee, pointing with a nod. "Maybe ten miles by the high trail of the Apaches."

"But you're not an Apache."

"No, Navajo," he answered.

As Pahee ate the meal the trader soon put before him —beans and lamb stew—he took in the immediate sur- rounding. This was indeed a trading store. He recognized familiar paper packages of coffee on the shelves. The cans and cans of fruit with pictures that always made him hungry when he went to such a store with his mother looked back at him from shelves upon shelves. There must be sugar too, somewhere, and bags of flour, and tobacco, cigarettes, and matches. Yes, this was the trading store Curly and Claw had talked about.

Pahee watched the owner moving about. He could not be absolutely sure yet whether the man was the Dutchman or not. He seemed to be a kind man, though. His hair was light, his round cheeks pinkish. His laugh was friendly, and he was generous with food for strangers. Pahee liked this man.

His eyes were blue, not blue like Curly's, but grayish blue, kind and dark. The only Dutchman he had ever known, as such, was Von Cronemeyer, who had come to the Navajo reservation years ago and married Pahee's aunt, Ta Hes Bah. He was old now, and his cheeks wrinkled and his hair white, but the eyes were the same.

"Are you the Dutchman, and is this your trading store?" Pahee asked at last.

"You've got me right," the man laughed. "Are you hunting a Dutchman with a trading store?"

"Yes."

"Do you have Dutchmen where you live?"

"One."

"What's his name, and where does he stay?"

"Name's Von Cronemeyer. He got married with my aunt long time. They live at Ganado. Sometimes Winslow."

"My name's Meyer, myself," laughed the man. "I'm just half the man your aunt married." Pahee looked puzzled.

"People in this section mostly call me Dutch, but I was born in Pennsylvania. My granddad was born in Holland," he said, reaching for his straw hat on a nail over the water jar. "You'll camp with me tonight, won't you, or are your folks camped back on the trail somewhere?"

"I'm alone," answered Pahee, "and I want to stay a day—maybe two."

"Suits me and Mutt fine. We don't have much company here since the mines shut down in the Silver City country, do we, Mutt?" Meyer put on the warped straw hat. "You can watch me do the chores," he said. "There's a hutch of rabbits down by the cow's stable that you never saw before, I'll bet."

Pahee stepped outside the little store. The dog followed him, rubbing a friendly side against the boy's knees. Meyer closed the screen carefully. "Can't stand flies," he explained, "nor the millers that come in at night in herds as soon as I light my lamp."

Pahee walked close beside this man. He did not feel shy, nor ashamed as he often felt with some white people. Meyer was a good man. Of this the boy had no doubt now, as he watched him doing the evening chores.

By bedtime, when the two had put their cots on the tiny, screened porch and Pahee lay looking up at the stars in the sky far to the south, he felt happier than he had since he and Chee had taken the sheep into the mountains months ago. Tonight he would rest, think, and plan. Tomorrow, maybe, or the next day, he would watch for the roan with the scanty tail and the man with the curly hair and pale blue eyes.

FIVE

LOOKING
HIM OVER

A sunrise behind Pahee, Curly was preparing for the day's ride down the crooked creek trail. At breakfast Chee had heard Claw jibe him about tending strictly to business.

"It's that trader you are goin' to contact, remember," he had said. "Keep clear of Silver City. Your friends there have stretched hemp by now, unless they're studyin' navigation at Alcatraz. And don't forget what a moll does in our business. You know firsthand."

Curly winced at Claw's last remarks. Chee could see the pale blue eyes glitter and the thin, square jaws push into hard knots near the ears.

"A bit of firsthand experience you've had yourself," said Curly, plainly struggling to control his anger. "As for the dames, I've been able to dodge their cutlery so far. Ain't no gal going to put her brand on me!"

Claw forced his face into a horrible grin at this. The scar stood out a heavy, blue, crooked welt. Chee felt half in sympathy with him. Whatever the subject of controversy, Curly, apparently, had taken an unfair advantage.

"As much for your own good as mine," said Claw calmly. "Got along pretty well before I throwed in with you. Could do it again, I guess." A long and tense silence followed this statement, as the two men looked at each other hard.

"Make it back here in a few days?" asked Claw, finally.

"Easy."

"Stick to your trail. You know your weakness for bright lights. I'd make the trip myself but I'm too easily spotted."

With Claw's final thrust stinging in his ears, Curly swung himself onto the roan and clattered away over the rocky flat toward the creek trail on his way to the trading post.

For some time after Curly had galloped away, Claw lay on his elbow with his low forehead drawn into a deep scowl. He chewed a sage twig and spit savagely. Yaqui had been around the flock and returned with a lamb to slaughter. Chee had gone to where the packhorse was picketed and moved her to fresh grass. Claw's horse was hobbled, but moved to the packhorse's grass, too. When Chee returned to camp, fresh mutton hung in a mesquite tree, and Yaqui was busy with his braiding in the thick shade of a dwarf cedar.

Chee curled up in the open near the pack saddle. For some time no word was spoken. At last Claw motioned to have his horse. Chee went for it, returning the still-hobbled animal mincing daintily along, with now and then a clumsy attempt at a trot that might have toppled him over.

Claw unlocked the hobbles, saddled the horse, and jogged leisurely down toward the creek trail. Chee lay a few yards from Yaqui, who scarcely seemed aware that Claw had ridden away. Presently Yaqui turned his eyes in

Chee's direction, meeting those of the boy in a straight gaze, and said in good Navajo:

"*Ya Te yay, Sihkis?*" (How are you, friend?) Then in fluent English went on earnestly:

"Redskin, if you are playing a game you have nothing on me. If you can speak English and can understand what I say, then listen. Keep your eyes open and don't move."

Chee made no sound, but his heart thumped.

"You are a Navajo. The best friend I ever had was a Navajo, my partner in Vietnam," Yaqui said, looking straight into Chee's eyes. "We had agreed if either one returned he would bring word to the family of the other. He died in Nam, battle at Mai Tho."

"Can I trust you, Redskin?" asked Yaqui.

"His name?" asked Chee, trembling.

"Yazzhie."

"My mother's brother!" exclaimed the boy. "The one Navajo killed in that place was my Uncle Yazzhie. A soldier came and told us!"

"He was my friend," said Yaqui. "He taught me how to cook the mutton. I cook it as he did, yet you refuse to taste it."

"For a good reason," added Chee quickly. "This flock belongs to my parents. You know how they came to be here."

"Yes," answered Yaqui, "but don't think me a man like Curly or Claw. Terrible men, both of them. Our lives would mean nothing if they knew we were deceiving them in any way. As soon as they can do as well without us as they can with us, they will put us out of the way. Curly seems worse even than Claw, though it is easier to like him. Both are desperate criminals. They hired me in Juarez to help them with their packhorse. I was running away from the Mexican gold mines. I wanted to reach Alamo and live with Yazzhie's people. That I still hope to do."

Yaqui looked long into Chee's eyes, then hurried on.

"Curly and Claw were hiding from Chicago officers. They went to Juarez. There they killed two men and a woman in a drunken fight. They robbed an old señora in El Paso and left her to die with a blow on her white head from the butt of Curly's gun. It was at Juarez that a white woman slashed Claw's face with a butcher knife, defending herself. All this I have learned from their own lips. I listen. They think that because my skin is different from theirs that my ears and brain are dull.

"We must keep on just as we are until the chance comes," Yaqui continued. "Then we must be sure, for if an attempt fails, we are dead that minute. We are dead whether we even make an attempt against them or not, as soon as they discover we are deceiving them in any way. Claw will not come back till afternoon, maybe. He always rides off alone when Curly leaves his sight. Curly plans to look over a place for the robbery and murder they are planning in a few weeks. That's where he's gone now. Some trader who lays in winter supplies for prospectors and trappers who come into the country in winter."

As fast as he could, Chee told Yaqui how he and his brother had followed the robbers. How he had gone ahead of the flock, pretending to come from the opposite direction;

how he had gotten into the camp, communicating with Pahee on the outside; and how, by now, his brother was at the Dutchman's store, "looking things over" for himself.

Yaqui was amazed at Chee's story and at the courage of the two brothers.

"If it was not for Curly, I could have taken Claw hunting gold and lost him," Yaqui confided. "Claw is crazy for gold, but Curly likes ready-made money and would rather ride the roan than tramp the gulches. I know a place where I could lead Claw and lose him for weeks before he could get out!" Yaqui said. Then in very low tones, he confided, "See these big ornaments and heavy tassel-tops on this bridle? Full of gold nuggets! So I am not the dumb Indian Claw and Curly think I am. And with you and your brother to help, unarmed as we are, we may be able to bring these men to justice and return your sheep to your family."

Toward noon, Claw returned from down the crooked creek trail. Yaqui and Chee had seen him far below the camp and had stationed themselves apart. Chee was some distance away, digging industriously among the sage and greasewood. Yaqui was preparing some of the mutton to dry on the stubby snags of the dead cedar. In fact, the cedar was quite covered when Claw rode up. Then Yaqui began frying mutton. He made flat dough-cakes that would follow the mutton in the hot grease and cooked coffee.

After a time, Chee sauntered up with his arms full of barky yucca roots. These he laid on a rock in the sun. The three soon surrounded the stone where Yaqui had piled the crisp, brown cakes, and the noonday meal was on. Chee ate no mutton, as usual, but he did not turn down the fried bread and black coffee, to say nothing of the wild garlic he had added to the table.

By midafternoon Chee had pounded the yucca roots and had the basin of water piled up with foamy suds. Claw watched carelessly. When Chee began washing his hair, Claw sat up. The thick lather covered the boy's black hair. After some scouring and a rinse or two, the boy's hair was as shiny and smooth as silk. Then Chee took off most of his clothes and washed them. Claw motioned the boy to fix a basin for him, and was soon covering his own black hair with this desert shampoo.

Claw seemed really pleased with himself after a good cleansing, and motioned Chee to keep some on hand for daily use. Yaqui took little notice of what was going on, but worked on a square, braided watch ornament.

SIX

TWO MEN

Pahee had nevor sccn thc sun rise except over a mountain range, but after the night's rest on Meyer's porch, he woke just in time to see the sun actually leap out of the flat horizon to the east. It startled him, and he wondered what was the matter with the sun that it hurried into the sky without warning.

The Dutchman saw Pahee looking and laughed.

"Your sun at home has to climb a mountain before it can get up, don't it?"

Pahee answered that it did, and that it took it longer to do so.

"When the sun touches the top of the porch I get up," said the man. "I'll get breakfast after I milk the cow and feed the rabbits. You might as well stay holed up till I come in."

Pahee heard Meyer leave the house. Wide awake now, and refreshed by a cool night's sleep, he began planning his campaign. He had a notion to tell the man everything he knew as soon as they sat down to breakfast. But maybe the trader wouldn't believe it. Pahee decided instead to buy some shoes first and give his silver ring or bracelet in exchange. It might be best to say nothing about Curly. Curly might kill the man right away if Meyer let on he knew anything. Maybe even kill them both, and then what would happen to Chee and the sheep—and Meyer's dog. And yet, surely this white man could protect himself. Besides, he ran a store and must know a great deal. He was almost as tall as Curly and bigger. Still, Curly had a gun—two guns—and belts full of ammunition. But Curly didn't want to kill the Dutchman this time; he just wanted to look the place over now, and buy cigarettes and stuff. If only Curly's horse would throw him off and break his legs! Pahee felt confused about what to do.

When Meyer called Pahee to breakfast a few minutes later, the boy was as undecided as before. But as Pahee washed his face in the pan outside the door, his reasoning seemed to get cleared, and he asked questions fearlessly. He found there were no towns near the trader's store, that a place some miles off was named Silver City, and that the country around was full of old silver mines and prospectors' holes. Meyer showed Pahee a pile of silver ore.

"You can take all of it you can carry when you go home," he said, laughing.

Then Pahee showed the trader his silver ring and bracelet, explaining that an uncle had made them and had even cut and polished the blue stone sets.

"You can have them both for shoes for Chee and me," he said. "I came for that."

"The ring is enough for two pairs of shoes," Meyer said. "Two pairs at ten dollars each makes twenty dollars, don't it, son?" asked the man, "and your ring ought to be worth that. That's a good turquoise in the set, and it's well made."

Pahee watched the man's face. This was an honest

man, honest like his father and his uncle Yazzhie—and Chee and himself—and maybe even Yaqui. He decided he would tell this man everything he knew. A good white man's advice could be the best thing in the world.

The breakfast table at which Pahee was seated was square-topped and heavy. It was made of boards smoothed and polished by hand. It was large enough for four, but only dishes for two were laid. Bacon and biscuits and milk gravy steamed in dishes in the center. Meyer poured a tin cup of coffee for each, then sat down.

"Wade in on the grub, son," he said in a pleasing way. "These biscuits didn't turn out so well, but your teeth are good."

Pahee thought of Claw's flinty biscuits that Chee had brought him, and wondered if the white trader could eat one so hard.

"Old Mutt here has to have his breakfast from the table, too," the man said, dipping a biscuit in the grease of the bacon and handing it to the dog in dainty bites. "He's about the only company I have at mealtime, and he's always right on the spot he is now when the table is set. See that fan-shaped place, smooth as glass, on the floor behind him?" Meyer indicated the spot, "He made it with waggin' his tail."

Pahee laughed, then asked: "What kind of a dog is he?"

"Half police, half bull," the man answered proudly, "and he's as smart a dog as a man needs anywhere." Here Meyer gave Mutt a bacon-biscuit sandwich. "He can tell if a person is good or bad whenever he sees one. He can spot 'em; never fails. I'd trust that dog's judgment of a man at first sight rather than my own when I'd known him six months." Pahee looked surprised.

"See the way he stood, friendly-like and tail a-goin' lazy when you stood at the screen yesterday? That told me you were a square-shooter better than I could have told myself."

Pahee swelled with pride. He patted the big dog, setting the heavy tail sliding back and forth on its smooth arc again.

"Knows how to treat a gentleman, kind and sociable," Meyer added, "but he'd take the other kind by the throat and never let go till it thundered. That's the bull. A bull dog is a stayin' son-of-a-gun."

"Does he kill your rabbits?" Pahee asked.

"Never touches them nor the cow and her calf, but he don't like a hog"—Meyer gave Mutt the last piece of bacon—"unless it's cured and smoked."

Such friendly, intimate conversation had gone on during the meal that before breakfast was over Pahee had told Meyer his main reason for visiting him. The man listened intently. Pahee detected no fear in the trader's face.

"The man coming here soon is Curly. He is a spy to look things over, buy something and go away," Pahee said, trembling. "Then they are coming in a week or two, maybe three, and kill you so they can carry all your stuff to their den in the Ladrones."

Pahee was almost panting when he finished the details, including Curly's vow to kill the trader if the tobacco was bad—and that he would be sure to buy it, for he was out of cigarettes.

Meyer's calmness reassured him.

"He'll be riding a roan horse," said Pahee. "Thin tail."

"How does he look, this Curly?" the trader asked.

"Tall as you, maybe, not so heavy. Eyes pale blue, kind of green. Never have seen him close, but Chee says his eyes are not level, this side higher than this side," he explained, indicating right and left.

Meyer went to the tiny safe behind and under the counter, and brought out a piece of folded paper. Opening it, and spreading it before Pahee, he said:

"Look like either one of these?"

The paper was a reward notice for two criminals, with pictures of the men, wanted by Chicago and national officers.

Pahee was amazed.

"That's Claw, see his hand? Claw is Curly's partner. One hand gone, all but thumb and one finger, just like this," Pahee held his left hand up with three fingers doubled out of sight.

"This other bird does look crooked-eyed, a little, don't you think?" asked Meyer.

"Looks like it, maybe," answered Pahee, scanning the wrinkled paper.

"Ten thousand dollars reward each for capturing them," said Meyer, tightening his jaws. "Your Curly 'll be joggin' in here before long, likely, in time to look us over before dark and have supper with us afterwards."

The trader sat, apparently undisturbed, while Pahee told him everything else that had happened. Then, as if in friendly return for the confidence, Meyer told Pahee how he had come from Pittsburgh three years ago to make a home in the desert for his wife. "Tuberculosis, they said."

Pahee saw misery in the man's face.

"But in this hot, dry climate she can live and be well again. The doctors are sure she can." The man spoke hopefully, even joyfully.

"I worked in the smelters there," he began again. "We were building a little house and were happy till the smoke, dust—everything, I guess—worked together to make her sick; very, very sick," he explained.

"I left her with my mother in Pittsburgh and I came here. Everything you see around the place I have planted or built for her," he added proudly. "She can come by early fall. By late fall, the doctors say she must be away from there if she is to live."

Pahee's eyes were full of sympathy. He patted Mutt's head tenderly. He could see sympathy and understanding in the eyes of the big dog.

Presently the trader rose from the table, saying, "I have the money to send for Hilda and to buy the winter's stock for the store. I have worried much that sudden death, or some accident to me, might keep what I have saved from ever reaching Pittsburgh. Nobody but me knows where the money is, nor suspects that I have it. Come with me, son, to its hiding place. If anything should happen to me before I can send it to Hilda, you are to carry the tin box to Silver City and put it into the hands of the postmaster there."

Meyer looked relieved as he led the lad toward the east wall of the lava grotto and continued, "They might burn the store and my body, but still the money would be safe here."

Pahee was surprised that a white man knew how to hide his valuables as securely as an Indian would.

"Your secret is safe," said Pahee earnestly. "I would do what you ask."

At the top of the little lava cliff a few minutes later, the trader and the Indian boy clasped each other's hands with a fervent grip.

"When I make a promise I keep it," Pahee said simply, and in that wild desert above the tiny oasis in which lay a little home, a pledge was sealed that set a heroic heart at ease, and made a trusting Indian boy a man.

SEVEN

TWO KINDS
OF PEOPLE

Pahee helped about the table, and soon all signs of a breakfast in the little store had disappeared. The trader went over his shelves, pushing things back and making space for new goods he would buy before winter. The shelves were quite bare but for a few common varieties of canned goods, some crackers and cookies. There were also a few packs of cigarettes and tobacco. Pahee wished the trader would hide them. He thought once or twice that he would suggest it, but maybe the man would think of it himself.

From time to time, Pahee sauntered leisurely out of the store to return presently and make himself useful. Two pairs of heavy-soled shoes lay on the counter. Pahee had fitted one pair to his feet. The larger pair would be right for his brother. However, the lad found little enthusiasm in his purchase, not even in the fact that the ring alone paid the cost, with two silver quarters left over in change. He wondered that Meyer placed the small safe on the counter near the window, leaving it partly open.

"Don't you think Curly will come here?" Pahee asked, with his eyes directed plainly at the safe.

"I look for him before sundown some day soon," said the

trader, taking binoculars from a black case and placing them on the table. "With these I can see him miles away. At fifteen miles I can tell the color of his horse," he said proudly, "and I might just make out that funny shade of blue he has for eyes at five," he laughed.

But Pahee kept up his watch. He knew nothing of white man's binoculars, but he knew his own eyes, and from time to time swept the sloping country to the north as far as he could see.

Sometime after a lunch of bread and milk and a bit of dried beef, Meyer picked up the binoculars and went outside. Pahee followed to see the man put them to his eyes and slowly sweep the country in a wide circle.

"The old glasses can beat a man's eyes a hundred miles," Meyer said. "Since I learned to use them, I've never been without them."

"How did you learn?" Pahee asked as they returned to the little store.

"Flying for Uncle Sam," Meyer answered, as he replaced the binoculars.

"In Vietnam?" inquired Pahee anxiously.

"Korea," answered the trader. "Sometimes over the water, when you couldn't tell exactly what country was under you, and didn't care so long as the country or the ocean stayed under and didn't fly up and hit you in the face."

Pahee looked puzzled. Finally he said softly: "My uncle, Yazzhie, he was in Vietnam."

"Your uncle?" said the white man.

"Yes," replied Pahee. "He never came home. My grandmother won't believe he is dead. We heard that. But my grandmother says my Uncle Yazzhie will come home—maybe."

The trader was surprised at the knowledge and understanding this native boy had of the conflict not so long ended and that men still reluctantly spoke of. But as the afternoon wore on, Pahee learned that Meyer had been a U.S. Army flyer; that most of the time he had flown a scouting plane; that he had escaped injury entirely, save for a broken leg and arm in a crack-up he and his partner had near Seoul, the capital of South Korea.

"Not so skillful, my lad," Meyer assured Pahee in answer to the boy's expression of praise for the white man's skill, "just plain lucky. Many a better flyer than I could ever be is still under the wreckage of his ship, somewhere, or buried in the soil of a country far from home."

The trader was silent for a moment. Pahee watched the man's face eagerly, and waited. Mutt wagged a sympathetic tail. Hour after hour the man picked up the glasses and again went out to scan the horizon. Pahee watched intently, following the binoculars in their slow, steady sweep of the arc to the northwest. Now the glasses retraced part of the arc, stopping at a point Pahee judged to be straight north. He looked in that direction, straining to see as far as his eyes could reach. He detected no object. Still Meyer held straight and firm on the point.

Then he said calmly, "A traveler—horseback—about twelve miles up. Might be a roan. Ought to make it here in a couple of hours. Depends on how much of a hurry he's in."

With these words, Meyer reentered the house, Pahee close behind him.

"He'll be hungry and dry, whoever he is," said the trader. "You can carry a fresh bucket of water from the spring. The jar's getting low."

Pahee grabbed the tin water bucket and was off down the lava gulch to the spring, returning in a few minutes with a full bucket. His practice with the tin cup had helped.

"Guess that'll be enough for three," the man said as he emptied the bucket into a stone jar and replaced the cover. He continued, pointing to items as he talked.

"Here's cheese, and crackers, and sardines, and pickles, and canned tomatoes he can choose from. If he's hungry as he ought to be after a day's ride, he can make out. You see these dishes under here?" he asked, pointing into the hollow back of the counter. "They're for people that want something besides paper boxes and tin cans to eat out of, the particular sort," he said with a grin. "City folks."

Pahee went behind the counter. He had thought it solid like a long, overturned box. It looked solid from the front and from the end not against the wall. But it was hollow, with shelves and compartments. There were the few dishes, with knives and forks and tin spoons; there were a few half-gallon tin buckets of molasses, some cakes of yellow soap, and part of a coil of rope.

Pahee admired the neatness with which the trader had arranged his stock, but he couldn't keep his mind off Curly.

"You could be the waiter, couldn't you?" asked the trader. "That is, in case anybody wants to eat?"

"Yes," Pahee answered readily.

Another look through the black binoculars and Meyer said, "Roan horse all right. Cantering along at a fair clip, but he'll be nosing down for a stop before long, as the flying squad used to say.

"Don't be nervous, son," Meyer said, seeing that Pahee was worried. "Nothing at all to be scared about. I've had all kinds of customers sit on that high stool and eat crackers and cheese. I get so lonesome during the summer months I'd be glad sometimes if Old Nick himself—that's the devil, not your Saint Nick, mind you—would come in and chat a while, and eat cheese and crackers."

The trader replaced the glasses in their leather case and slid it behind a row of canned tomatoes, stepping carefully over Old Mutt so as not to wake him.

"You see, Buddy," said the trader, addressing Pahee jovially, and slapping his shoulder, "it takes all kinds of people to make up a world. Folks like you and me—and Old Mutt—and folks that ain't like us. Folks like us stick together, don't they? Especially when the flying gets rough?" Meyer looked Pahee in the eye straight, and with meaning. Pahee understood.

"I stick with you and Old Mutt," Pahee said in a low, steady voice, offering a hand that did not tremble.

Meyer took it heartily. "Buddies!" said the trader earnestly.

The sun was an hour or more from setting when Curly threw his rein over a post near the trading store and made his way leisurely to the door, open but for the screen. Old Mutt was there in a flash. He growled savagely, and his lips curled with menace. The hair on his back stood up like the fin of a great fish. He braced his feet firmly and looked the stranger wickedly in the eye.

"Call off your pup," the man said, his hand moving inside his jacket, "before I bite him."

"Mutt, you childish old sinner, come here! Come here!" said Meyer, laughing and taking the dog by the collar. "Here, buddy, take him."

Pahee dragged the dog to the corner, pushing him gently to the floor, where he lay sullenly. Curly came in.

"The dog's childish as an old man with rheumatism and a brood of bothersome great-grandchildren," said the trader amiably.

Curly's bluish eyes swept the neat, almost empty shelves.

Pahee took in every detail as he stood with one foot tenderly stroking the dog's back.

Curly helped himself to the water and drank greedily. Filling the cup again, he carried it to the counter and climbed to the high stool.

"What could you find for a man to eat?" he asked. "Been on the road for a week, hungry enough to eat an Apache squaw, papoose and all," he said, with a look at Pahee that Pahee didn't like. Really, the man's pale blue eyes were not set straight. He knew, now, exactly what Chee meant: his eyes were indeed wicked.

"Stock's pretty low right now," said the trader apologetically, "but I can fit you out with cheese and crackers, and salmon or sardines. Here's pickles and canned tomatoes and fruits."

"Set it out," said Curly, leaning his elbows on the counter and humping his back till his leather jacket gaped, showing a bit of the gun under his arm.

Meyer placed dishes in front of the customer while Pahee handed things from the shelves, placing them conveniently on the counter and laying the can opener beside the tomatoes. Pahee remembered the molasses, and set a jar of it on the counter. He recalled how delicious molasses was, and wished for some himself.

Before Curly began to eat, he asked for tobacco. "Ain't had a decent smoke since I left Flagstaff," he said.

Now Pahee looked for trouble sure enough, though the man, really, wasn't acting like a criminal. Ten thousand dollars for each one of them, the paper had said. Curly was one of the men, that was plain enough. Of course Claw was the other—his hand showed clearly in the picture. Pahee wondered if the trader had noticed that Curly looked like the picture. He hadn't seen him looking at the man very much. Of course, Meyer was busy waiting on him.

"Hard to get good tobacco, sometimes," said the trader, as he placed the only two packs of cigarettes he had on the counter, and the one small pack of tobacco.

Curly's lip twisted as he turned a pack over in his hand. His pale, bluish eyes glittered. Yes, one was lower than the other. How plainly Pahee could see it!

"Hangin's too good for a man who'd sell that kind of stuff to honest smokers," he said insolently, slapping the pack on the table and beginning to eat. Pahee stood behind the counter.

Meyer laughed good-naturedly.

"Guess you're right at that," he said. "My stock's about run out, but I'll be filling her up in a couple of weeks. I freight my goods from Silver City. There's not much business here in the summer, but when the trappers and the free-lance miners and the wildcatters drift in here in the fall, business is pretty good." Meyer busied himself about the shelves and counter as he talked.

More than once, Pahee had seen Curly look toward the safe. In fact, he had seen him glance at it as he stood at the water jar by the door, then turn his funny eyes quickly away.

"When'll the stock be full?" Curly asked. "My outfit'll be wanting good stuff, and lots of it, before long."

"That's fine, that's fine," said the trader, taking the tin cup to the water jar and filling it.

"Mighty glad to have you get it here," he went on, bringing the tin and setting it near Curly's elbow. "Mighty glad to give you the. . . ."

Here, Meyer pounced like a mountain lion, and before Pahee could quite realize what had happened, Curly had been thrown to the floor and lay stretched out, face-down on the floor, with Meyer on top of him.

Mutt had also leaped, and in an instant was snapping at Curly's ankles. "No, Mutt!" the trader yelled. "Go lie down!" And the dog, both snarling and whimpering a little, obeyed.

The trader remained calm as he held the rustler's arm twisted upward and behind the robber's prone body. Curly's own face was red, however, and he was cursing a blue streak. But every time he struggled to get away, the trader's grip held firm, and the robber would yell even more.

"The guns, buddy," said Meyer. "Take his guns away, carefully. And then bring the rope under the counter. Quickly."

Pahee obeyed.

"Tie his feet together. Can you do that?"

"You hold, I tie. I tie goats, never get loose," he replied.

Curly struggled, kicking his legs furiously and bringing Mutt snarling to his feet again.

"Don't do that," said Meyer, just as calm as before, "or I'll let Mutt chew on your boots a while."

"Lousy dog," cursed Curly, his face still red and his angry eyes somehow now looking green. "You'll regret this, old-timer."

"Not likely," said the trader. "Buddy, tie his other hand now; then we'll do the other one and connect them to his feet. That'll keep him."

Pahee obeyed. Then they half-carried, half-dragged the still-cursing Curly outside.

Soon, Curly was lying on the ground outside the store, his arms were tied securely behind him and his legs bound tight at the ankles. His two guns and his cartridges lay in a heap inside the store.

Pahee and the Dutchman stood back to look at their handiwork, and Pahee asked him, "How did you do that? How did you get Ches Chilly down on the floor so fast?"

"Ha! That's something else I learned in Korea. Never had to use it till now though. Teach you sometime, maybe."

"I like to learn that."

"So it's a deal. But for now we have other things to do.

Water the man's horse, buddy," the trader said cheerfully.

This made Curly struggle again, violently, wrenching and twisting till his face was purple. He cursed in whispers, in growls, in shrieks. "You rat!" he said, seeing Meyer standing a few feet off. "Rat!"

"The less you say, Curly, the better for you," said the trader. "You can go peaceably, from your own choice, or I'll slug you and you will go peaceably from my choice. Whichever way it is, young fellow, you go! Don't forget that." Meyer spoke with disarming calmness. Curly began to blubber.

Pahee led the roan up. Surprised to see the man crying, he turned with a look of genuine concern and said, "He having a fit? Looks like it."

The trader had to laugh. "Just about right, buddy, I'd say offhand. Fit to be tied."

"Here's the hobbles locked to the saddle," Pahee said. "Chee says Claw carries the key, but maybe not this time."

A search of Curly's pockets produced the key. Pahee had the hobbles off the saddle in a few minutes. The roan nibbled the dry, scanty grass.

"Wonder how a horse hobble would work on a man?" asked Meyer. "They look enough like handcuffs to be a pretty good substitute. But we'll keep the ropes, too, for good measure."

Curly lay straining, cursing, bellowing, in turn. Old Mutt stood beside his master, ready again, eager for action. The sun was close to setting.

"You stand guard, buddy," said Meyer, "you and Mutt.

I'll go to the little pasture for horses."

Pahee felt brave and useful. Meyer was soon out of sight, in the pasture a short distance down the lava valley.

By threatening and cursing, Curly tried to make the boy untie the ropes. Failing in this, he tried pleading piteously. This strangely touched Pahee, but he pretended not to hear. Then Curly offered the boy great sums of money. "I've got sacks full of money—thousands—hid in the mountains. You can have half of it if you'll untie my arms."

Pahee looked far away to the south. "Sheep better than lots money," he said.

"I've got sheep, too, Redskin, I've got whole big herd."

The boy shook his head. "Claw and Yaqui have sheep, not you. Soon they not have, either."

Then Curly raved, he roared and swore. Pahee had never heard such wicked words before. "Untie me! Untie me, you Redskin, or I'll kill you and that rat of a Dutchman and cut your hearts out!" Pahee tried to pay no attention.

It was growing dark. Pahee lit the lantern and sat near the man. Meyer came up with two horses.

They found the hobbles as convenient, and safe, as real handcuffs, and by eight o'clock Meyer and Pahee were on horses. Curly, tightly tied into the saddle and his ankles shackled together under the roan's belly, was between them. They rode past the little corral, where Meyer got off his horse and opened the gate.

"Old Bossy can look out for herself and her calf while we're gone," he said, "and Mutt will take care of the rest."

As if he understood and approved, the dog turned tail and trotted back to the house, where he lay down in front of the door.

It was nearing nine o'clock, and the full moon was rising in the east, by the time the trader and the Indian boy headed down the sagebrush slope for Silver City. Between them was Curly—cursing, pleading, and blubbering in turn.

EIGHT

A PROMISE

Most of the late afternoon of the day Curly had ridden away from the camp Claw spent in polishing up his person. Chee had set the example. A huge pile of pounded yucca root lay on a flat stone in the sun. Claw had even taken an armful and gone to the creek, returning toward sundown just as Chee was going for water. Yaqui had delicious mutton stew simmering in the coals, but the sooty coffee pot stood empty. If Claw had been annoyed that the coffee at noon was pale and taste- less, what would he be at supper? Yaqui had done his best in making the stew, and there were cold, flinty biscuits of Claw's own making several meals back. They must be used, for supplies were running low. The packhorse would travel lighter than he had for some time when again the robbers were on their way.

Chee returned with fresh water, and Claw hunched himself along the ground to a place nearest the food. His mean look of disgust that his huge tin coffee cup held only water would be hard to imagine. But to the surprise of the others, Claw had no complaint, and the meal was finished with few words.

"Something's got to be done about supplies, and that pretty quick," Claw said as he washed down his last mouthful of mutton with a gulp of water. "Injuns can live on nothing and like it, maybe. White men have to eat—and drink and have their tobacco." Yaqui grinned. Chee made no sign that he even suspected what had been said.

"Indian tobacco good!" said Yaqui. "No smoke-um. Chew-um."

Chee had to grin at Yaqui's pretense of Indian lingo. Yaqui offered Claw a pinch of the dry, tough, sagey leaves.

Claw stuffed the leaves into his mouth and took a sip of water. He sat with his lips closed, his hands hooked over his knees and a cynical look of expectation in his gaze down the crooked creek trail.

"Might get the habit in time," he said at last to Yaqui, "in a lifetime, you might say. Bitter, and salty, too." He kept on as he tried to munch the tough, tangy leaves into shape. "Guess after all it's nature's own make, and at that no worse than the stuff Curly says is made out of burnt molasses, alfalfa hay, and creosote—I'd say with a barn-yard thrown into the vat for bulk and flavor."

Claw ended his opinion of poor store-bought tobacco with a renewed effort at subduing the wild variety that seemed to grow bulkier and more unmanageable in his mouth. Yaqui gazed unconcernedly at him from time to time and went about straightening the camp for the night. Chee was changing the range of the packhorse. He had to change her stake often, for Claw's horse would feed no-where else but by her side.

When Chee had laid Claw's bed and taken his own place near the pack pony and Claw's saddlehorse, Yaqui said:

"Tomorrow hunt Indian tea, me."

"If it's as bad as Indian tobacco, it ought to be good,"

Claw answered cynically, and rolled, fully dressed but for once clean, onto his bunk near the campfire.

Nights are usually cool, even chilly, in the mountains of New Mexico, though days may be hot and dry. Claw had learned that though a place near the campfire might seem a bit too warm for sleeping at first, it would be very comfortable as the night wore on.

Yaqui removed some of his clothing and washed his head and face in the yucca root. Using the coffee pot, he made thick suds that covered his black hair with creamy-white foam.

"That dummy that's with us knows his suds, if he don't know much else," said Claw, rising on his elbow and drawing his talon finger across his mouth. "Can't say so much for this stinkweed I'm trying to chew, but I'm for the dummy's soap substitute."

Yaqui grinned with his head turned and his hands scrubbing away at his hair.

"Curly ought to be joggin' in in time for early supper one day soon," said Claw. "He'll bring coffee and tobacco with him, and we'll pull up stakes here and make for the Ladron gulch pronto," he added, blowing the sodden mass of Indian tobacco from his mouth and dropping back on his bunk.

Chee lay awake far into the night. He had looked forward each evening at sundown to the signal. The absence of it gave him a feeling of loneliness and anxiety. The sheep were bunched and were resting quietly. They had grown accustomed to his fear at their approach, and paid no attention to him anymore. Though this attitude made Chee's deception much easier, still he felt the sting of being forgotten so completely. He knew Pahee would signal at sundown on the day of his return, and tried to put away his worry.

The quiet that descends so completely on the desert when night is far advanced now enveloped the little camp. The packhorse was sound asleep, resting the tip of her nose on the ground and breathing heavily. Chee alone seemed to be the only living thing awake. But sleep would not come to the boy whose day had been so full of surprises and confidences. His heart was so full of the secrets and sights Yaqui had described to him in Claw's absence that his eyes would not close.

Now his little brother—perhaps many miles away— might need him terribly. Might meet Curly and be killed. Maybe even the trader might be a bad man who would kill the boy and rob him of the silver bracelet and ring. Thoughts that Chee had never dreamed of before now frightened him. He decided that he would move nearer Claw and Yaqui. Of this he immediately thought better. The moon was full, and Claw, seeing someone moving, might rise and fire—and kill—just as he had one night when Pahee's own pet goat wandered from the flock up near the campfire. To Pahee, that was as much a murder as the killing of the white-haired old señora in El Paso.

Chee lay close beside the horse. He could count on animals, wild or tame. But men, they were not easily understood. Of Yaqui, Chee had no fear. He would have gladly crept nearer to him, but dared not move because of Claw.

Daybreak came at last, and Chee, worn out with the night's restlessness, fell only then into a heavy sleep.

Breakfast was over when he woke. The packhorse was

grazing at the outermost edge of her circle. Claw was saddling his horse as Chee came up. Yaqui was helping with the hobbles.

"Curly's got the key, but you can pry the spring up with this crooked blade," Claw said, handing Yaqui a knife. It was a queer knife with several blades. Some looked like keys, it seemed. Yaqui would like to have examined the implement, but didn't exhibit any curiosity.

"Keep the sheep pretty close," said Claw to Yaqui as he swung into the saddle. "If Curly finds things right, we'll be shiftin' gears before you know it."

With this remark, Claw jogged down the crooked creek trail as he had done before. Yaqui sat down at his work, straightening a few strands of sorrel hair to weave the design in a fob he had begun. Chee saw Claw round the little point and drop from sight before he started his breakfast. Remains of a meal still lay on the stone near the campfire. He gazed at some mutton scraps.

"Fried an extra," Yaqui said as soon as he could safely venture speech. "Thought you'd like it just as Yazzhie used to cook it. *Shosh Begay!*" (son of a bear) he swore, pointing with his lips in the direction Claw had taken. "I thought I could take him last night, but I don't think he ever sleeps."

"*Chinde shosh begay!* (devil son of a bear)," swore Chee.

That Yaqui knew how to swear in Navajo made Chee sure that what the Indian had said was true about Yazzhie. That he had called Claw a "son of a bear" pleased the boy. No viler name could be called by a Navajo. He could, himself, add but "devil" to the sentiment Yaqui had so eloquently expressed.

"Every day he expects to ride down the creek till he

meets his friend," said Yaqui. "They ought to get back by supper."

"What if no coffee?" Chee asked and laughed. "My soap is good, your tobacco 'stinkweed,' he said like that," the boy added, spitting vigorously.

Yaqui and Chee doubled over with laughter.

"In Mexico they drink liquor—vile stuff," Yaqui explained, "made from mescal plant."

"I know that drink," said Chee. "Apaches make it. Makes them mean!" he added with a shrug.

"If we don't get coffee, I'll get some willow leaves and cook them. The juice is black like coffee," Yaqui said.

"And not the tobacco? The trader, maybe he's out of his tobacco, like Claw and Curly," Chee added.

Yaqui and Chee idled in the camp. Yaqui's stories of war in a foreign land, and of the appearance and customs of different people, helped to pass the time, yet both were restless. They must get away from these robbers. Yaqui and Chee could do that easily enough. But the sheep. Neither one would think of returning without them. No. Something must be done with the wicked men who murder, rob, and eat the herds of honest shepherds.

"A weed that grows near Indian tobacco kills those who chew it," said Yaqui.

"I know a weed that makes long sleep, sleep like dead," Chee said with enthusiasm, "then wake up, been someplace, tell about it."

Yaqui grinned.

"At fiesta in one Pueblo once," Chee explained, "one Pueblo man take lots coffee made with that weed. He went to sleep fast. Everybody stayed in that house, for he's going tell where he's been when he wakes up. People they wait long time. Then one man made more of that coffee and everybody took it and they went to sleep." Chee was excited. "Then they were all asleep. The Pueblo man woke up. Told long, long story. Nobody heard it." Chee laughed. "That what my father say."

"Ever see any of that coffee weed growing in this country?" asked Yaqui with apparent unconcern.

"Saw some up on the Apache trail," Chee replied, "where an old camp had been. Back that way, long way."

"How long?" asked Yaqui.

"Half day I get there and come back, run lots."

"Go," commanded Yaqui.

With a look of inquiry, and an answering nod from his friend, Chee was off, up the slope and headed for the old trail several miles away.

Yaqui grinned. "Quick to understand before you tell him," he said to himself, "like Yazzhie. Not afraid, too, like him."

For some time Yaqui sat with his head bowed. He recalled Yazzhie, his best friend. That Yazzhie had lost his life in a strange land made him sad. Tears came, and soon made rivers down his cheeks.

"I will keep the promise we made that day," Yaqui said aloud and fervently. "I will keep it for him. He would keep it for me."

NINE

RESTLESS CAMP

Time went slowly for Yaqui. Alone in the camp, he found no heart to work at his bridle. He went around the flock several times, partly to pass the time but mostly to watch from vantage points for Claw and Curly. He hoped it would be late enough for Chee to have returned without being missed. But it wasn't.

Claw galloped in near sundown alone. Chee had not returned.

It was plain that Claw was out of sorts and worried. Out of sorts because he was hungry and without coffee and tobacco. Worried because he had not met Curly. He could not have missed him . . . anyway, Curly had not arrived. He should have made it in, even with a pack animal. Claw cursed his partner freely and angrily. He never should have allowed him out of his sight. No doubt the fool had taken the opportunity to get to Silver City. "Pretends he knows good tobacco!" Claw exploded. "A woman's picture on the box makes a stogie taste like a Havana's best to him. The fool! Give me another fistful of that musty hay you've got, Yaqui."

Yaqui handed over a generous mouthful and Claw tamped it in. For a while he was busy with the unpleasant substitute. Yaqui was uneasy, but went about as usual, preparing the meal. To the mutton stew with wild garlic and green shoots was added Indian potatoes baked in the ashes and fried bread crisp and brown. The coffeepot stood in its accustomed place. Into the hot water it held, Yaqui put a handful of willow leaves, some bark, and a few juniper twigs.

"If your coffee is as rotten as your tobacco, Indian," said Claw presently, "you needn't fill my cup more than a quarter full. Where's that dummy? He could help a little."

"Here a little ago," answered Yaqui. "More yucca get 'em maybe."

The sun was down. Yaqui delayed serving supper, hoping every second that Chee would appear. Claw's horse had hobbled off to the packhorse as soon as freed of the saddle. This would warn Chee that Claw was in camp. At last, Claw drew up to the food steaming on the thin flat stone. Yaqui poured some liquid from the pot. The two had just begun to eat when Chee dashed up with two rabbits dangling from his shoulders.

"How do you suppose he got 'em?" asked Claw in surprise. "How did you, Dummy?" he asked Chee with pointing motions.

Chee explained by using sign, with elaborate gestures, that he chased them, threw a crooked stick; they dodged; he chased and threw; the rabbits ran and dodged. Claw openly lost interest in the simpleton, and fell to indulging in the more satisfying business of cursing and reviling Curly. It was only through Claw's abuse of his partner that Chee learned that Claw had ridden miles down the trail to meet Curly, and that Curly was nowhere to be seen; that as Claw had half expected, the man had probably ridden on to Silver City.

"Girl in a cafe down there smiled at him, Curly thought, and the fool's been wanting to go back to see if she's still in the same cafe, with the same grin stuck on her face, six months later," Claw said with disgust. "The fool! What's worse, the girl was grinnin' at *me*, not him! Gimme another dose of that coffee substitute of yours, Yaqui," Claw said with a sweep of his cup toward the pot. "Substitute like that ought to put chicory out of business. Don't have any coffee taste, but it's hot and wet."

Yaqui laughed a little.

Chee drank the beverage with his fried bread, cleared up the table, and went to re-picket the horse. The sheep gave him no trouble at any time. Contented with feed and water in plenty, they were fattening and growing beyond his expectations. But he was not content himself. He had watched for smoke signals from his brother in every direction at sunset and found none. He would listen during the night. At least his trip to the old campsite on Apache Trail had yielded well. He didn't know for sure what Yaqui had thought of, but he believed they were both of the same mind. Tomorrow he would know.

The night was as endless to the boy as the previous one had been. What if Pahee, like Yazzhie, should not return? No signal. Tomorrow he must go for Pahee. Fear that the boy might encounter Claw or Curly made Chee's body burn with anxiety. Tomorrow. Would the endless night ever pass, could he risk going near Yaqui to get a single word of cheer or encouragement? No. He dared not creep to the side of his new friend. Worry and thought kept him awake for what seemed like hours, but at last Chee curled himself near the horses, and slept.

Despite getting little sleep, early day found the boy wide awake. Nobody was stirring. And with morning came clearer reasoning. Maybe Pahee had stayed at the trading store, waiting for Curly. Curly might go to Silver City first. Chee knew that the shortcut through the malpais flats could bring one to Silver City, leaving the trader's far to the east. Apache boys had told him at school how other trails led from the old Apache road to different points. Curly could have taken one, gone to Silver City first, and returned by way of the Dutchman's store. That could account for Pahee's delay. He would speak to Yaqui about the idea as soon as he dared.

Later as the two Indians watched Claw gallop vengefully down the crooked creek way, Chee explained his theory to Yaqui.

"Curly might cut across the lava beds, but I don't think so," Yaqui said. "He could keep the regular trail, pass the Dutchman's on his way to Silver City, taking in the trader on his way back. That would delay your brother, too."

Only when Claw was well out of sight did Yaqui ask, "Did you find it?"

"Lots."

Here Chee drew several large, blue-green leaves from the buckskin bag at his waist, under his clothing.

"Grows all around where a sweat-house must have been," said the lad gleefully. "More around there."

"This ought to do unless he's too tough," Yaqui said with a straight look into Chee's eyes. "Do you get the idea?"

"Had it long time. It will make sleep, Curly and Claw," answered Chee with as steady an eye as Yaqui.

"We drive our sheep back ourselves," he continued. "Leave them sleep like Taos man. Wake up, tell long story, nobody hear."

Yaqui laughed.

"We can't let men like Claw and Curly loose," said Yaqui seriously. "They've told me of their crimes—women, girls, men; robbed, mistreated, murdered. The old helpless señora at El Paso. Murdered for nothing."

Yaqui's dark eyes then shot fire. "In war we murdered too, maybe...," he said, tightening his eyes as if to shut out the scene of slaughter. "But everybody was killing then. We had to kill to save our lives—to save everything the people loved, they said."

Then Yaqui opened his eyes, saying with a firm voice, "But not now. These men murder for greed, to have their lawless way, for revenge. They killed the old señora for no reason at all, unless angered at so few pesos to steal in her casita." Yaqui looked savage. "They should be carried—or driven—back to El Paso and given to the sons of the old señora. There they would get punishment!"

Chee, surprised at Yaqui's bitterness and savage manner, touched him kindly on the shoulder.

"If Curly does not come tonight, we will take Claw's guns when he sleeps," said Chee. "You know how to use guns."

Yaqui smiled, a little sadly.

"Better than Curly or Claw," he said. "They hired me to drive the packhorse. When they would reach their rancho, they said, the mare was mine. I had no gun. They probably think I don't know how to use a gun. I had no knife either. I had nothing but a few nuggets of gold hidden in the ornaments. They said the bridle, they would buy it when I got it finished. I work on it, but it is never finished," he said with shrewd, half-closed eyes.

"They paid me no money yet. Then I found out what they are. Outlaws hiding from capture. Cowards. Afraid to face honest men. They surround themselves with others like them. In their hiding place in Ladron Mountains, they think they will be safe to carry out their wicked trades," Yaqui said, with an ugly expression now in his dark face, "but they shall not reach that place. I have waited for my chance. It will come—maybe tonight, maybe tomorrow. 'Mañana' as Mexican people say."

"Are you brave?" he asked Chee.

"Yes," replied the boy. "There are things worth more to me than my life. Keeping my word to my parents, doing what I promise, my brother Pahee, working honestly, and being a good shepherd."

When evening came again, Claw returned, once more alone. As he neared the camp, Chee was gathering wood some distance away. Yaqui was starting supper. Claw galloped up. He threw himself from the horse, uncinched the saddle, and heaved it to the ground. Then, hobbling the horse and striking him sharply with the bridle, Claw sat heavily on a stone near the fire.

Yaqui, as usual, waited for Claw to speak. He did,

presently, with a guttural explosion that was terrifying. Chee heard him as he came up bearing a thick load of sticks and dry sagebrush. Chee never had heard words used in such wicked phrases as Claw was using them. Yaqui, apparently unmoved, went about setting the food before the angry man. The coffeepot simmered by the flat stone near the blaze. As Claw began to eat, Chee and Yaqui remained quiet, sitting respectfully and discreetly apart.

"Pour me some of that black stuff you call coffee," ordered Claw.

Yaqui filled the tin. Claw blew his breath into the cup occasionally and took a drink. He was hungry, doubly so, he said, with no tobacco since Curly left. At any rate he ate greedily, and, finishing his meal quickly, he downed the coffee cup as the final rite.

"Now some of that stinkweed you call tobacco, Yaqui, and I'll be fixed up right," Claw said, sneering as he held his hand toward Chee's friend and confidant.

Yaqui gave him a generous handful, and Claw stored it away in his mouth. For some time, the three then sat silently, watching the sun drop behind the last range.

Chee watched intently for a signal. Yaqui appeared morose and sleepy. Claw chewed gingerly, swore occasionally, and at last lay down. Darkness came on, and still there came no signal. The moon rose, round and red and near. Chee moved the packhorse's rope and returned to camp expectantly. Claw appeared to be asleep. Chee spread the man's bed.

"Your bed. Here it is," said Yaqui.

No answer.

"Here, Claw," he said again, shaking him roughly. "Your bed." Claw made no move, but was limp and breathing peacefully.

Yaqui deftly unbuckled Claw's belts. Chee sprang to his side instantly and grasped both guns. Claw still didn't move. Yaqui removed the knife and other items from the pockets of Claw's heavy leather coat.

"He sure did let us have guns," gasped Chee. "You give him kill-man-leaf with your tobacco?" he asked hopefully.

"He's only asleep," said Yaqui with a grin. "There was medicine in that cup, not coffee like ours."

Chee almost laughed with joy.

"One gun on you, one on me," Yaqui said, buckling a belt above his muscular hips. Chee followed the example, feeling proud to carry a pistol, but a little afraid of it.

"We will hide him and his horse," said Yaqui. "If Curly comes, we will say, 'Claw is not here. Rode after you. Silver City, maybe.' "

Chee ran for Claw's horse, taking the knife to unlock the hobbles, and hurried back. Yaqui quickly transferred the horse's fetters to Claw's unmoving legs. Meanwhile, Chee saddled the horse.

Claw was not a heavy man, but, limp as a wilted weed, he was hard to lift up and drag across the saddle. Even so, Yaqui somehow lifted him up, and Chee tugged from the opposite side. Soon they had Claw on the saddle, his arms and head over one stirrup, his legs and feet over the other. Tied securely as the man was by the rope he had carried on the saddle, there was no danger of his falling off.

"I'll lead the horse," said Yaqui. "You bring the pile

from his pockets, and the coffeepot. Don't spill it."

Across a narrow point among sagebrush, yucca, and cactus, the two made their way. Then they dropped into a gulch which they followed for some time. At last, entering the mouth of an arroyo that led up a wild slope, Yaqui took the way to the west.

The arroyo headed high up among piñon and cedars. Here, in an abandoned prospector's shack, they unloaded their prisoner. Claw mumbled some complaint as they tumbled him to the dirt floor, but was soon snoring again.

"When Curly comes, he will be armed; so will I," said Yaqui.

"And me," said Chee. "I shot a gun once. I can do it good, maybe. Try hard."

The moon showed past midnight. Claw was getting restless and beginning to come to, but Yaqui offered the tin cup to his mouth, and he drank and was quiet again.

"If Curly was coming tonight, he would have been at camp before this," said Yaqui. "Curly, though brave and boasting when he is armed, is afraid in the dark. I have seen that. All murderers are scared when they can't see behind them," he went on. "I will go back to camp to look for him. Are you brave enough to stay here?"

"Yes," answered Chee, "to stay, or go, I'm brave enough. Claw's legs tied, hands tied, no gun. Asleep hard. Wake up, give more medicine, lots, maybe."

Yaqui laughed, and so did Chee, and then Chee was alone with his captive and his own thoughts.

Yaqui made his way down the trail they had come. The going down was easy, and he reached the camp in less time by half than it had taken to get to the hiding place.

The moon was getting low. The sheep were quiet. The packhorse was asleep. There were no other signs of life at the camp. Evidently Curly had not returned.

Gathering up some food, Yaqui once more made his way back across the cactus, up the gulch into the mouth of the arroyo, and on up the slope. He reached the prospector's shack just at sunrise. Chee was waiting outside for him.

"Got here just in time," Yaqui said, nodding toward the sun, now showing full. "Nobody there. Packhorse gone to bed. So too the sheep."

"He likes to sleep," Chee said, nodding in the direction of the doorway. "When he wakes up a little, swears, I give him another drink. He will sleep now—maybe long time."

Yaqui eyed Chee accusingly. "Not too long, I hope."

"No. He be OK."

Yaqui produced cold mutton and fried bread and the two sat outside the shack door to have their breakfast.

TEN

A STRANGE
TRIP

No sooner had the meal begun than Chee sprang to his feet.

"Watch!" he called, pointing to a thicket on the slope of a small mountain west of them and south of the camp.

"Smoke! Wait and see!" he said, pointing in the direction. "High and thin!" he said. "Pahee! I will go?"

"Yes."

Away dashed Chee across lava flows, through arroyos, and up prickly slopes. No need to hide so carefully now. Curly was away, and Claw asleep. Leaving the camp some distance to the left, Chee made his way toward the thin column of smoke, which was now fading. His feet flew over the sharp cactus and flinty rocks. His shoes had no soles, but his feet felt no discomfort as he raced to make his brother's camp before the smoke—his guide—entirely disappeared. At last, he stopped in a thick clump of greasewood when he smelled smoke, for the first time, and made the call. The answer came immediately, and from a thicket of sagebrush close by, Pahee came in a run and stopped before him, raising a cloud of dust.

Chee threw himself on the ground, grasping Pahee's knees in a wail of joy.

"My brother! My brother! You are back again! I thought maybe you were dead!"

Pahee put his hand on Chee's head.

"They hear you at camp. Be careful!"

Then Chee told Pahee that Curly had not come home yet. That Claw had been very angry; that at last Yaqui and he had disarmed Claw and had him hidden some distance off; and when Curly came, they meant to catch him, too, for Yaqui had a gun now, Claw's best one, and so did he.

Chee talked fast; Pahee waited. When Chee had finished, Pahee told him Curly was not coming back, that he was in a jail in Silver City. His horse's hobbles were now on him, and officers from El Paso were coming for him. They wanted Claw, too. Pahee told Chee that he had been to Silver City with the trader who had captured Curly, and that he had brought two pairs of shoes and had come horseback with the trader to a place a mile west, where the trader waited now.

"Bring the man to the camp!" said Chee. "I run for Yaqui. We will bring Claw to camp, too."

At this the two boys sprang in opposite directions, bounding over the rough ground like deer.

With as much exciting news as each had to tell the other, it would seem that the two brothers would have been too happy to think clearly. But they were not. Shortly after noon, Yaqui and Chee, with Claw mounted on his horse, came into the camp. Pahee and the trader were waiting. Claw was talking eloquently. He was making gestures of real grace. He had no other use for his hands, as Chee led the horse and Claw's legs were hobbled together in the stirrups. The trader and Pahee had food prepared.

Yaqui and the trader talked earnestly, eating as they stood. Claw insisted on telling of a marvelous journey he had taken, and of a strange country he had traveled where gold was to be had for picking it up, and beautiful women smiled at one on every side as they served food, coffee, and tobacco. He stressed the coffee and tobacco in that strange land. It was much better than that offered by merchants in Chicago or El Paso.

Yaqui offered Claw food, which he took politely, praising its excellence and preparation. When an occasional sign of returning reason appeared in Claw's conversation, he was allowed a drink of coffee from his tin. To him now, the tin cup was a silver stein, flagon, or mug, according to whatever name he gave the beverage.

In Claw's pockets were found accounts of crimes in different cities. These accounts, torn from newspapers, gave names of suspects and other bits of information. The trader and Yaqui questioned Claw concerning these, writing names and information as he freely gave it.

"Might be some truth in what he says," the trader said.

"It might be well to keep a record, anyway," said Yaqui. "If it helps to clear up any other mysteries, or to bring other criminals to justice, it will be worth all the trouble. In his waking time Claw will talk freely. As the effects begin to wear off he will crave more. We have plenty to last for some time."

Yaqui's explanation interested Meyer. The mutual experiences of the two men drew them close together in this desert land so far from war and conflict in Asia. They talked earnestly. Meyer explained the reward offered for the capture of the criminals. Divided equally, it would give each of the four a generous sum.

"I came to help you boys with Claw," said the trader. "Pahee stood by me like a brother. We could have cashed in on just Curly but we wanted both of the rascals," Meyer said, laughing.

It was finally thought best for Chee to go with the trader to help escort Claw to his partner in Silver City. Horses would be available now. Chee should have the trip.

"He's been around very little, but he's intelligent, keen and trustworthy, brave and courageous. He comes from a good family." Here Yaqui could not keep from giving the trader a short sketch of his comradeship with Yazzhie.

"To live as one of Yazzhie's brothers is more to me than a reward in money," Yaqui said.

By evening, Meyer and Chee, with Claw between them, were making good time down the creek trail. Claw would talk fluently and eloquently at times, then drift into muttering that apparently meant nothing. Occasionally Chee offered him food. Sometimes he ate, sometimes he refused it, but the drink he always accepted. When asleep on his horse, he slumped over the front of the saddle, but awake he sat straight. Like a platform speaker, he would tell of his travels and adventures in strange lands the like of which could exist nowhere on earth. At other times he frankly answered questions concerning his crimes as if these too were a part of his marvelous experiences. Then he would sleep heavily, dream another adventure, and tell it on waking.

With such a companion as Claw, it would seem one might travel a long journey enjoyably. But the trip might also become very boring. So it did to Meyer and Chee. Long before they reached Silver City, the two were talking pleasantly and hearing no word of the adventures Claw might be telling with really eloquent language.

The sun was an hour or more above the eastern horizon when Meyer and Chee, the talkative companion between them, rode into Silver City and turned Claw over to officers of the law.

At a barn they saw their horses cared for, and then found a place where they could eat.

At the bank, the reward was divided into four equal parts.

"Yaqui said he wanted none of it," Chee explained. "Only the pack pony they promised him. But no reward. Pahee said 'No money for me.' I will take one part for Yaqui. He can give it to my Uncle Yazzhie's mother from her new son."

The officers and Meyer could not understand the attitude of persons who refused money rightfully theirs.

"Put the other two parts to the credit of Yaqui and Pahee jointly," said the trader, "and we'll thrash out the details later. They deserve an equal share with us."

Just before Meyer and Chee left for the return trip, the trader wired money to his wife in Pittsburgh. They took off for the trading post. Claw's and Curly's horses had been turned over to Chee and the trader. As they jogged out of Silver City, each led an extra horse behind.

The trip to the trader's store was a pleasant experience.

On the way, Chee learned much of Meyer's history in the armed forces in Korea as well as the man's efforts on his return to the business of making a living. Chee in turn exchanged experiences.

His Uncle Yazzhie had never come back from the war, despite his grandmother's mute sorrow and her firm belief that he still lived and would return. He told of the joy his parents would feel at the condition of the sheep and lambs when at last they were brought to the home herding grounds.

"Sheep are better than money," said Chee. "Sheep will last a long time. They will grow and have many more. Money never stays long. It gets less all the time. Gone right away. Nothing left."

Meyer was astonished at the profound philosophy expressed by this Indian boy. They jogged on in silence. At last Chee said, with a sweep of his hand, "Many sheep could live here. Lots of range and water. It is better than much money."

Meyer laughed heartily at the lad's explanation.

"You may be right at that," he said. "Could be."

Not far up the long slope, Chee could see a green pocket in the lava gulch and knew they must be nearing the white man's home. Sometime later, the two halted at the gate. Chee wondered at the neat building and beautiful surroundings. Old Mutt lumbered up as the two got off their horses. The old dog's tail beat first Meyer, then Chee. The trader turned the horses into the little pasture, and he and Chee entered the house for food and rest till morning.

ELEVEN

HOME
RANGE

Relieved of Claw, Yaqui and Pahee began immediately to make plans to break camp. Yaqui was so happy at learning, after many weeks' wondering, that he was so near to the people he had set out to find that he was anxious to be away. He rubbed and patted the pack pony fondly.

"Mine, now," he said. "Never had a horse. In Mexico I dug for gold-rock!" He went on. "Horses are better, and sheep, and people that you belong to."

Then for a time, Yaqui said nothing. Pahee respected the silence, and went about preparing food for the two. As anxious as both were to be herding the flock, they could not leave for home until Chee's return. At supper that evening, it was decided to head the flock toward their home range next morning. Pahee would graze them along slowly, and Yaqui would wait at the abandoned camp for Chee.

"We can come up with you before too dark," said Yaqui as he tightened the pack straps on the pony, now spitefully expanding her sides in resentment. He patted the horse affectionately. She nuzzled an apology on his shoulder. "I never had a horse till now," he said proudly.

Yaqui watched the herd disappear into the mesquite

and greasewood to the west. Pahee led the packhorse behind him. With their noses toward home, the goats and sheep traveled briskly along, bent on making time. They had covered several miles before Yaqui and Chee overtook them at dusk. The two were on horseback, and led an extra horse.

"This is yours," said Chee, dismounting from Claw's horse and putting the reins of Curly's roan into Pahee's hands. "Officers at Silver City gave them to us. Yaqui to have this horse and saddle," Chee said gleefully, stroking the mane of Claw's former horse. "Meyer said he's got too many horses already. Now Yaqui got two."

The supper camp that night was the happiest in many days. Their horses grazed near, and the herd was glad to rest. Until far into the night, Chee and Pahee listened to the incidents Yaqui told of their Uncle Yazzhie in a land far away.

"When I reach his people, I will tell them that Yazzhie's actions were always brave, and that his thoughts were always for his comrades first. One night he asked us to promise that we would take a message to his family. These were his words:

" 'Tell my mother, Chee Mal Yazzhie, I am her son in far away land. If I do not come home, another must take my place in the hogan. Do as your son Yazzhie asks you, Chee Mal. I have said it.' "

Yaqui repeated the message several times that night before the three stretched themselves near the campfire to sleep.

Many pleasant days and peaceful nights passed before

the flock and the three shepherds reached their home at Alamo. The tribe was summoned immediately. Men and women and children sat in respectful silence about a circle on the soft desert soil. At one edge stood the hogan of Chee Mal Yazzhie. Piles of dry sage, cedar, and greasewood lay on the outer edges.

As the moon rose, three chosen youths brought torches from the hogan and touched them to the waiting fuel. The fires sputtered, then rose in crackling white flames. Old Nah-tah-ne stepped from the hogan of Chee Mal Yazzhie. Holding a hand above his greying head, he explained the object of the meeting.

"Two of our bravest youths have brought honor to our tribe." Then he said with a commanding voice, slowly and with dignity, "Chee and Pahee, stand with me."

The two boys hung their heads and made their way to the old chief's side.

"Their courage has brought great honor to us. Their bravery, and their faithfulness to the task their father set them to have, brought great honor to themselves, to their parents, and to their tribe. They have returned with their family's flock and with horses and with paper saying much dollars."

The old chief drew a thin, shapely hand across his brow and went on.

"With our own two brave sons has come a stranger. He comes from far away. He brings news from another of our brave sons. One who will not return." Then, in eloquent huskiness and graceful gesture, old Nah-tah-ne repeated the message Yazzhie had given his comrade that day in a

country beyond the Big Water toward the setting sun.

Old men sat about the circle with bowed heads. Women wept, wiping their tears with hard hands, or the edges of their heavy shawls; children, hushed and wide-eyed, made no sound.

At last Nah-tah-ne went on. "Chee and Pahee, show the stranger the way here."

The two youths went off into the hogan, returning immediately with Yaqui and Chee Mal Yazzhie.

"This strange youth was sent to Chee Mal in place of her own son who cannot return," Nah-tah-ne said. "He cannot speak all of our language yet but he is now a Navajo. From this night, Yaqui is Chee Mal's son. His name is Tso Begay Yaqui."

At this, the white-haired old woman clasped her thin arms about Yaqui and wept softly. The grandmother said, "My son, you will be happy again among the people. We have had great sings for those who have returned from Vietnam. The white man say they are sick from shell shock and diseases. The medicine man has special ceremonies to purify them and wash away the evil effects of killing."

"This son brings to Chee Mal the comfort of a good son to his mother," Nah-tah-ne said solemnly, "and much riches."

As Yaqui stood with the old woman's arms around him, and with Chee and Pahee beside him, he said in fair Navajo:

"My tribesmen, my brothers, my mother! You are better than big riches. I have said it."

The fires had burned out, and the moon was nearing

the western earth, when men and women and children, after much feasting and joy, scattered over the desert to hogan, flock, and loom they had hurriedly left when Nah-tah-ne called them to the ceremony.

Shik'éí Shidiné'é, biłha'azhigí
Shiłhózhǫ́ hooghandí nanasdzáá
Shiłhózhǫ́ hooghandí nanasdzáá
'Ahéhee, Níłch'í Diyinii
Hooghandi nanasdzáá
Shikékłáádę́ę́' bił hózhǫ́
Shi'álákłeedę́ę́' bił hózhǫ́
Shintsíkéés bił hózhǫ́
Shitsíís bił hózhǫ́
Nizhónó hooghandi náá'shá
Nizhónó hooghandi náá'shá

My family, clan relatives, those I have
    been raised with,
I'm happy to be home,
I'm happy to be home.
Thank you, Great Spirit,
I am home again,
My feet are happy,
My hands are happy,
My thinking is happy,
My soul is happy.
It is good to be home again,
It is good to be home again.

THE AUTHOR

Maurine Grammer, author, anthropologist, teacher, and appraiser of Indian arts and crafts, has lived for more than fifty years in the Indian country of the Southwest. She draws on years of experience, friendships, and patient listening to write with insight and accuracy. Mrs. Grammer is held in high respect by several generations of Navajo people.

THE ILLUSTRATOR

Fred Cleveland, the illustrator, is a Navajo born at Ganado, Arizona. He began making pictures on the dirt floor of the family hogan at age five. He was educated at the Albuquerque Indian School and the American Academy of Art in Chicago. Cleveland has won numerous awards, and his paintings are in major museums and private collections throughout the world.

DATE DUE

HIGHSMITH   # 45102